THE PROPOSAL

TB MARKINSON

LET'S KEEP IN TOUCH

One of the best parts of publishing is getting to know *you*, the reader. My favorite method of keeping in touch is via my newsletter, where I share about my writing life, my cat (whom I lovingly call the Demon Cat since she hissed at me for the first forty-eight hours after I adopted her), upcoming new releases, promotions, and giveaways.

And, I give away two e-books to two newsletter subscribers every month. The winners will be able to choose from my backlist or an upcoming release.

I love giving back to you, which is why if you join my newsletter, I'll send you a free e-copy of *A Woman Lost*, book 1 of the A Woman Lost series, and bonus chapters you can't get anywhere else.

Also, you'll receive a free e-copy of *Tropical Heat*, a short story that lives up to the "heat" in its name.

If you want to keep in touch, sign up here: http://eepurl.com/hhBhXX

CHAPTER ONE

I'M HERE.

My finger hovered above the screen momentarily, and I had to stop it from shaking before I could send the text. My plane had just made it to the gate, and though the little I could see through the window suggested Heathrow Airport in London was nearly identical to every other airport the world over, it was still impossible for me to pry my eyes away until the buzz of an incoming text stole my attention.

For real this time?

I laughed, picturing the excited look on Glory's face as she sent this. Actually, that wasn't exactly right. What I pictured was the grinning profile of a dark-lidded Egyptian princess, which was the avatar she used in the chat room where we'd met four months prior.

No, not a singles chatroom. It was an online book club. Yes, we're both literary nerds.

From the day I first joined the group, Glory stood out. She always had the snarkiest comments, and I'd be lying if I tried to claim that kind of thing didn't get me a little bit hot and bothered. In the good way, though not everyone in the group agreed. Truthfully, Glory had a way of riling people up. Secretly, I admired her spunk. I was never brave enough to pipe up when there was controversy on the horizon. And if you don't think online book clubs are a hotbed of squabbling and strife, well, you haven't spent much time around passionate readers.

As the seat belt sign went off, and every person on the plane jumped to their feet at once, completely blocking me into my window seat for at least another ten minutes, I turned my attention back to the conversation at hand.

Yes, for real.

My inability to make it to London in person had become something of a running joke between us. I'd started as a sales manager for Books! Books! Books!, or Triple B as the company was known in the biz, right around the same time Glory and I started chatting. One of the perks of the job was the promise of travel, as Triple B was in the process of snapping up struggling independent bookshops at bargain basement prices around the globe. Yet, each time a trip to the UK had been planned, something had happened.

In July, my boss had gone into premature labor two hours before I was supposed to leave for the airport. I'd been forced to scrap my plans so I could take on an important client meeting in her absence. August brought a pilot strike, and every flight I tried to book got canceled. I made it to London in September, but not the one I wanted. It was the London in Canada. In October, the entire New York area was hit by a record-breaking hurricane that shut down the airports for a week. I kid you not.

But now, November, it was finally happening. All I had to do was survive my meeting with Cleo Braithwaite first.

A shiver worked its way through me, and it wasn't due to the steady rain pelting the window beside me.

Ms. Braithwaite was the owner of a bookshop that had been in operation since the days of Charles Dickens. My objective today, and there was no way to sugarcoat this, was to get her to sign on the dotted line. Braithwaite Books would be the jewel in Triple B's crown, and closing the deal would make me the queen.

Other companies had tried to gobble up the shop, but Braithwaite had stonewalled every single attempt. The woman had a certain reputation in the book world, and if only a tenth of the rumors had a whiff of truth, well... no wonder I was feeling the beginnings of an ulcer. The woman terrified me.

I wasn't exactly known in my department as the

shark. Order was my specialty. Spreadsheets. Dotting all the Is and crossing all the Ts. I was usually sent in after the wooing was done, making the deal official with signatures and initials on the paperwork. Whether it was my personal life or my professional one, courting wasn't in my wheelhouse.

How on earth had I gotten myself into a situation where in order to win the woman of my dreams, I had to hammer out the business deal of the century, too?

You see I'd had a sleepless night not too long ago, during which I'd taken a serious look at my bank account and realized if I ever wanted to meet Glory in person, I needed my company to cover the price of the airfare and hotel. In a flash of brilliance—not that I necessarily condone making do-or-die career moves at that hour—I crafted an email to my boss explaining all the reasons I was the perfect person for the Braithwaite deal and then tapped send before I could over-think it.

It had worked.

I wish even one of those reasons I gave my boss had actually been true.

A new text flashed on my screen.

I can't wait to meet you, Carol.

Carol is not my name. It's Marley. What can I say? My birthday is in December, and my dad was a huge fan of Charles Dickens. But since I was named after *A Christmas Carol*, I use the name Carol as my online handle. It's also the name of a famous lesbian literary character, and it can come in handy when gauging the prospects for romance with other sapphic literary nerds. If a woman makes a reference to the Patricia Highsmith book when I introduce myself, chances are she's a lesbian or bi.

As for Glory? It was the first thing she asked. Besides spunky, she's also direct.

The knowledge of our impending meeting carried me on a cloud all the way through passport control and to baggage claim, where I retrieved my rolling suitcase, inside of which, along with the usual business attire, I'd packed my killer date night little black dress, a pair of high heels that made my legs look a mile long, and a particularly nice set of underthings.

You know, just in case.

I reread the text about meeting me no fewer than fifty times during the fifteen-minute ride on the Heathrow Express. Each time, my insides turned the consistency of warm maple syrup as I contemplated the bobbed black hair of the tiny avatar I'd been staring at longingly since the moment we'd met.

By which I mean the day I worked up the nerve to slide into her DMs after weeks of hunting down every one of her comments in the book group. Until then, I'd read and admired in secret, but that day she was experiencing a particularly bruising pile-on for a statement about Shakespeare that was obviously meant to be ironic. Not that any of those philistines understood her humor. I finally plucked up the nerve to send her a private message to cheer her on.

The rest, as they say, was history.

Messages zipped back and forth over the pond at lightning speed. Every morning began with a greeting, each night with sweet wishes for good sleep. In between were the hundreds of little observations and jokes that pushed me ever deeper in love with someone I had never met, whose face I hadn't seen except as a one-inch square, caked beyond recognition with makeup for Halloween. But in only a few more hours, I would be meeting Glory in the flesh. The thought filled me with hope and existential dread.

Yeah, the dread came as a surprise to me, too.

This latest relationship in the cloud was basically the pinnacle of my romantic history on this planet. Oh, sure, I'd dated before, but never for long or seriously. This time, unconventional as it might be, was certainly the real thing.

My head was so lost in thought I barely noticed the train had stopped moving until the announcement of Paddington Station echoed in my ears. Though it had been a peaceful ride, the doorways were jammed by frazzled and grumpy-looking travelers desperate to get out of the train. By the time my foot reached the platform, I felt like I'd walked through a tornado. I moved to the side to fix my hair and skirt. I'd heard everyone in London went out of their way to be polite, but so far, my experience had suggested otherwise.

Many of the people in the crowded station were dashing toward different platforms, presumably to transfer to another train. It took all my concentration to finally locate the arrow pointing the way to the exit. I'd been in Britain for less than two hours, and a massive headache was forming behind my eyes. Luckily, it was only a little after eight, and my appointment at Braithwaite Books wasn't until nine, giving me time to drop off my bag at the hotel. After that, I wanted to grab a bagel and some coffee.

Could you get a bagel in London? As a New Yorker, I might die without them.

Once outside the station, I sucked in a deep breath of fresh air, enjoying the scent of the rain that had stopped while I was on the train. The pavement below my feet still had that slippery feel after a downpour, and the clouds above pressed down just so, like getting a celestial hug, while streaks of sunlight poked out here and there.

Everything simply seemed so special and charming. Was that because I was in London, a city I'd always wanted to see? Or because I was finally on the edge of all my dreams coming true? After all the bad luck, I'd been starting to think fate was stepping in to say, "No love life for you!" That was all going to change tonight.

As if to affirm how vastly improved my luck had become, a small cafe came into sight a few feet to my right. Stepping inside the restaurant, I scanned the bread and pastries, not spying a bagel. I didn't care.

My gaze fell on something even better than my original purpose. Something I would never order in the US, but I was in a foreign city, so my strict diet didn't count here, right? What one ate in London, stayed in London.

A woman behind the counter looked expectantly at me. I ordered a flat white coffee and a cinnamon Danish. After paying and tucking the receipt into my expenses envelope, I went back outside. Half a block later, I stopped at my hotel and left my luggage at the front desk. I'd requested an early check-in, but my room wasn't ready. It was probably for the best. I'd been traveling all night and still had a long day ahead of me. The mere sight of a bed might've done me in.

Back outside, a drizzle of rain splattered the sidewalk once again, and the streaks of sun were nowhere in sight. Pulling my umbrella out of my bag, I worked my way around the corner, leaving the hustle and bustle of the busy street and heading toward Braithwaite Books.

CHAPTER TWO

HAVE you ever walked into a place, feeling like you'd been there before? This was exactly what happened to me when I arrived at Braithwaite Books. As I pulled the door open, bells tinkled, and as I got my first full look at the interior, I was certain the sound came from a bevy of tiny fairies. Oh, how I wished I was a kid again. I wanted to spend the day browsing this magical place, which looked like the type of bookshop that only exists in the movies. It was nothing like what I'd expected.

To prepare for this assignment, I'd dug into the history of Braithwaite Books, and I'd come away with three preconceived ideas.

First: it would be a thoroughly out of touch organization that would rely on its famous name to keep it teetering on the right side of oblivion.

Second: Cleo Braithwaite would be an intimidating

force of nature. Since it was impossible to find a photo of the woman, not even a grainy one in a newspaper writeup about a charity event, I pictured a severe bun and thick spectacles.

Third: it would be a slog to get the owner to understand how much the publishing business was changing every day.

I was willing to admit my first assumption was completely wrong. This place was the opposite of stuffy. It was the type of shop created with the purpose of nurturing lifelong readers and helping children slip into the wonderful world of fantasy.

There were two women working that morning, and I needed only a moment of assessment to know my second assumption would be dead-on. One was a woman in the neighborhood of early thirties, like me, with a scarf pulling back her blonde hair in a way that made her look like a fortune-teller. Standing beside the counter, she bounced on the balls of her feet as if tap-dancing in her mind. I decided to nickname her Zelda and then dismissed her entirely, as there was no doubt her companion was the one I'd come to see.

With her stern expression and no-nonsense attire, Cleo Braithwaite must have been a schoolmarm in a former life. The type who never spared a slap of the knuckles with a ruler. My heart sank because when it came to signing a contract, Zelda looked a lot easier to convince. The schoolmarm sent a shudder through my body, making me bump into a display, nearly toppling a life-sized version of Wilbur and Charlotte from *Charlotte's Web*.

Zelda rushed forward.

"I'm so sorry." I tried to settle Charlotte, who was bobbing all over the place on a string that was threatening to wrap itself around my neck. "This is a lovely store."

"I'm glad you think so." The woman placed a hand on the giant spider, wrangling her into submission and saving me from a terrible death.

Behind the counter, Cleo was staring daggers at me, sharp enough to cause physical pain. I glanced back at Zelda, steeling myself for the unpleasantness to come. "I have a nine o'clock appointment with Cleo Braithwaite."

Zelda nodded as if she already knew that, but she didn't say anything. She probably felt bad for me, like I was being sent off to slaughter. I took in her flowing skirt and peasant blouse, which hinted at scrumptious curves underneath.

Knock it off, Marley! I told myself, forcing my eyes to look away. *You're spoken for. Kinda.*

I'd come all this way to meet Glory, after all. I didn't need to let my eyes wander when the perfect woman awaited me at the end of the business day.

Speaking of business, Cleo Braithwaite had disappeared from behind the counter and was nowhere to be seen. I couldn't decide if she was unaware of who I was or if she was being remarkably rude.

"Um, do you know if she's expecting me?"

"Yes, most definitely."

I glanced around, still failing to locate my target. I was beginning to suspect Ms. Braithwaite was spying on me from the back room, and this was some type of test to prove my worthiness to meet with her. I didn't know how to explain I wasn't the gauntlet type. If that was going to be a part of this pitch, they could count me out right now.

"Would you like a cup of tea?" Zelda asked, moving toward the back of the shop with a jaunty step. "I find I can't do the simplest of tasks without a proper cuppa."

Warm relief washed over me. I felt like I'd received a reprieve, even if only long enough to have tea.

"Yes. Thank you." There was a huffing quality to my words as I took ridiculously long strides to keep up.

Zelda led us to a small table, where there was an electric kettle, several mugs, and all the fixings for tea. It appeared to be available for anyone, customers or staff alike, to help themselves. For free. If memory served, the proposal I'd brought with me suggested installing a full-service cafe that could increase profits by twenty percent. No wonder Braithwaite Books was struggling financially.

After preparing two cups of tea, Zelda waved me to a cozy armchair on one side of the tea table. She lowered herself into the matching one on the other side. Meanwhile, I had my eagle eyes trained on the door to the back room, ready to pounce as soon as the mysterious Cleo reemerged.

"You're American." This wasn't posed as a question but a statement, although it was difficult to discern if there was judgment implied.

"Yes."

"Where from?" Her face lit up with possibilities, or so I imagined from the wonder residing in her eyes.

"New York."

"No, you don't sound like a New Yorker." She tapped her earlobe with a finger. "I'm picking up more of a Midwest accent."

"Uh, yeah, you got me there. I was born in Minnesota." I shuffled my feet, thinking I'd earned a bad mark for sure. Certainly no one in New York City had ever thought better of me after learning of my Minnesotan roots, hence why I nixed my accent as much as humanly possible. Was my exhaustion a factor, and I didn't sound like the sophisticated Marley I'd been perfecting, or trying to, for years? Zelda, however, clapped her hands together in obvious delight at my laziness.

"I thought so!" The woman raised her tea to her lips. "You live in New York now?"

"Yes."

"Why?"

For someone who dressed like a fortune-teller, the woman lacked the most basic of clairvoyance skills. If this exchange was the result of a causal run-in, I'd find it entertaining. Given that I apparently needed to solve some type of riddle before she would allow me access to her boss, I wasn't in the mood for games.

"I moved for work," I finally said, trying not to show my frustration, but I was beyond annoyed. No, scared was closer to the right word. While the tea was helping my nerves, it was delaying the inevitable. Any minute now, the schoolmarm was surely going to come out with a ruler or a paddle and send me crying back home, unsigned contract in hand.

The woman bobbed her head, and I couldn't tell if she was nodding to say she'd already put together I moved to New York for work or if she possessed psychic abilities and had picked up on the thoughts running through my head. I hoped for the former because if she knew the latter, my goose was cooked for sure.

"Will Cleo Braithwaite be joining us soon?" I swallowed hard. My boss had drilled it into my head how Britons expected punctuality. "I have a meeting with her that started two minutes ago. I don't want her to think I'm running late."

The woman studied the contents of her mug as if searching for the answer. "Give it another three minutes or so."

Wait. Was she actually reading the tea leaves? Was that even possible considering she'd used a tea bag? Who was this woman? Why was she intent on driving me bonkers? And, why couldn't I tell her to stop playing games?

I tried screwing up my nerve, but then I looked into her eyes again, and I couldn't do it. How could I yell at someone who seemed every bit as pleasant as her scary boss was bad-mannered?

Zelda closed her eyes, inhaling deeply before taking a sip of tea. Once she'd drained the last of her tea, a transformation came over her face. The fogginess was gone, and now all I could see was a sharp clarity.

In all honesty, it was a teensy-weensy bit intimidating, especially considering how unexpected it was. I was more in the dark about the situation than ever, but Zelda suddenly appeared to have all the answers.

"Right. Much better. Now that my tea is done, I'm myself again." She held out her hand, a trio of bangle bracelets clanging on her wrist. "I'm Cleo Braithwaite. I assume you're the woman Triple B sent to get me to sign over my family's legacy to be picked clean by American vultures."

CHAPTER THREE

"YOU'RE CLEO BRAITHWAITE?" I spluttered, my head swiveling from my fortune-teller hostess to the stern woman who was at that very moment emerging from the back, carrying not the expected ruler but a stack of paperbacks. "Then, who's that?"

"Sheila? She's my shop assistant." Zelda... er, *Cleo*'s expression shifted. "Oh, I see. You thought she was me?"

"I'm sorry. I guess I didn't expect the owner of such a London institution to be so—" My mind reeled, trying to come up with the right words for what I was thinking. The first two, *gorgeous* and *sexy*, were accurate but hardly appropriate, both because she was a client and because I had a date with another woman that very night. Was fate testing me? Or karma? Finally, I settled on, "Young."

"My mother was also Cleo Braithwaite," she

16

explained, "if that helps clarify things. I took over earlier this year when she retired."

"That makes sense," I said, wondering if I looked as dumb as I sounded. "Does that mean everything I've read refers to her?"

"Depends on what you've read." Cleo rattled her bracelets, calling attention to her outstretched hand. "I've introduced myself—twice, in a way—and you still haven't told me your name."

"I'm Marley Royce." I stuck out my hand, and Cleo shook it warmly, which was odd considering she'd accused not only me but my entire nation of being no better than vultures. I would have to get to the bottom of that, and soon if there was any hope of nailing this deal.

"Nice to meet you." Her gaze remained steady, capturing me and pulling me in despite whatever animosity she held against my purpose for being there. "Forgive me. I can't stop staring at your eyes. Such a deep blue."

"Thank you." My cheeks prickled with heat. I had no idea how to respond. Was this a tactic to put me off my game? "I like your scarf."

Seriously, I said that. And I did like her scarf. Her whole style really. But as comebacks go, that one was about as snappy as a bowl of soggy cornflakes. I was beginning to fear I was seriously outclassed, and all that exaggerating I did to my boss to get her to give me this assignment might end up getting me fired.

Cleo sat back in her seat, crossing her arms, appraising me with dark brown eyes. "How do we do this?"

I pulled my tablet out of my bag. "I'd like to go over some figures with you. Show you how Triple B—"

"Boring!" she shouted through cupped hands, her eyes daring me to so much as touch the on button, let alone begin scrolling through my carefully prepared presentation on the benefits of joining the Triple B family.

Fearful she'd chomp into my hand if I moved, I asked, "How did you picture this happening?"

"I'm not big on business details." She waved her hand in la-di-da fashion.

Which would explain the dire situation her shop was in and why Triple B wanted to buy her out. Except part of me suspected she was lying through her teeth, that the eccentric fashion choices and claims of not having a head for business were all part of an act designed to lure me in and put me at a disadvantage.

Her hand fell to her lap, like a baby bird who'd left the nest too soon. "I suppose you probably know that already."

Fuck. Had my internal thoughts telegraphed across my face? It was the truth, but I hated her sudden look of defeat way more than I should have, considering that was exactly how I needed her to feel if I planned to close this deal before dinnertime.

Get your head in the game, Marley!

"I think your family knows more about the business than any of us at Triple B," I said in a flattering tone, "given that you opened your doors in 1799."

"But it's not 1799 anymore, is it?" Her bravado faltered a bit, giving me a glimpse into her vulnerability.

I could work with vulnerability. Hell, I had a direct connection to that feeling, because *hello*, look up that word in the dictionary, and there was my shy face. I was still shaking from the way the schoolmarm, Sheila, was stalking the store like a lion guarding its territory.

Vulnerable was good. It gave me an opening if I could gather up enough courage to take it. All I needed to do was turn on my tablet and show her my spreadsheets. They told the story in full color. To me, at least.

A muscle in one of my fingers flinched, and Cleo's eyes pounced on it as if saying *I dare you to turn that thing on*.

Okay. No spreadsheets. I needed a different angle, pronto.

"It's not the heyday of brick and mortar, but that doesn't mean bookshops are dead."

"How'd you get your first name?" she asked, apropos to absolutely nothing.

"Marley?" I heard myself ask, sounding like I didn't even know my own name, let alone where it had come from. To the contrary. I'd known its meaning since I was a very precocious toddler listening to my father read from *A Christmas Carol* before bed. "My dad was a Dickens fan, and Mom disapproved of his first choice."

"Which was?" She leaned forward with rapt attention, as if she actually cared and wasn't seeking ammunition to pull a fast one on an adversary.

I hesitated, but couldn't figure out how telling the truth could hurt. "Nell."

"Ah." She nodded solemnly, appearing to be in complete agreement with my mother on this one. "Nell died in *The Old Curiosity Shop*. Not the most auspicious name you could give a baby."

"That was her line of thinking, yes."

"Then again, so did Marley. *Old Marley was as dead as a doornail*," she quoted, her voice deep and rich like a narrator on an old radio show. "Even the dog by the same name in that terribly sad Jennifer Aniston movie died if I recall correctly."

"Nine times out of ten, people think I was named for the dog despite being born years before the movie premiered." I couldn't help but laugh. I'd been reminded of both these details a million times. Or more. Hence, why I disliked going over my first-name history. I shrugged. "What can I say? Dad could be persuasive."

"Come to think of it, Mum had a dog named Marley many years ago." There was a sharp glint in Cleo's eyes as she studied me, like she was sizing up how much of my father's power of persuasion I'd inherited. "He's dead, too."

"I'm sorry." This conversation had me thoroughly confused. Was this how all sales calls in Britain went? I had to do something to salvage the situation. "Back to your shop—"

"Are you saying it's dead as well? I suppose that's why Triple B sent you. Are you like the Ghost of Christmas Yet to Come, *draped and hooded, coming like a mist upon the ground,* so you can show me the tomb with Braithwaite Books' name on it if I decide not to sign with you?"

I'd met dozens of bookstore owners and shop-keepers over the years, but never one so obviously well-read. Her perfect recital of Dickens astounded me so much it took me a moment to process the meaning of her words. "Hold on a minute. I'd like to think the offer I'm bringing is like the big goose showing up on Christmas morning."

"Does that make me Tiny Tim?" she asked, accompanied by a graceful arch of one eyebrow.

"Honestly, I have no idea," I admitted, too taken in by that mischievous brow arch to think clearly. "My analogy fell apart a while ago."

"Tell me what you know about London." A shaft of light came through the window, illuminating Cleo's cheek, and it was hard not to stare at her flawless skin. What type of soap and lotion did she use? If I started using both now, would mine ever look so good?

Uh-oh. She was staring at me. How long had I been sitting here without answering her question?

"This is my first time here," I scrambled to say, hoping I sounded more normal to her than I did to myself. "So far, I've only ridden the Heathrow Express, stepped inside a bakery for a coffee and Danish, and dropped off my luggage."

"That, and my shop, are the sum total of your London experience?" She looked flabbergasted.

"Your shop will be the highlight of my trip," I found myself saying, even as I was horrified by how honest and open I was being. But somehow, I couldn't stop and added, "I only wish I'd come here as a kid."

"Why's that?" She tipped her head to the side, weakening my resolve even more.

"It would have blown my mind," I whispered.

Cleo snapped upward in her seat, and I wondered where I'd gone wrong. "I have an idea."

"Oh?" My stomach tightened, but her dark eyes twinkled. I hoped it was reassuring merriment I was seeing, and not the look of someone about to pounce on their dinner.

"How about I play the Ghost of Christmas Past right now and show you the highlights of our fair city, all the ways it—and this shop—are simply too unique for the likes of Triple B?"

CHAPTER FOUR

I SHOULD HAVE REFUSED the offer on the spot, considering she'd nearly come right out and said she planned to reject the proposal I'd flown over four-thousand miles to convince her to sign, but instead I found myself offering a very wishy-washy, "I'm here for business, not pleasure," which, let's face it, was a lie.

I was here *because* of business, and I would take my job seriously, but my secret motivation behind the trip was to meet Glory. Sure, I found Cleo's company strangely charming, and part of me welcomed the idea of spending time sightseeing with her instead of working. However, there was no doubt in my mind I would find Glory ten times as lovely once we'd properly met. The sooner I closed this deal, the sooner I could make that happen. But somehow, I got the feeling Cleo wouldn't take no for an answer.

"Business is pleasure," she said, her tone a bit more tempting than it should've been. "Otherwise it shows."

As proof, she waved to the shop, which did have a lively feel. No customers, mind you, and that was a true shame because this place was the most enchanting shop I'd ever seen.

"You know, if you tried showcasing the shop on social media, people would flock to this place." I wasn't sure why I was telling her to do this instead of promising Triple B would make it happen, but I couldn't seem to help myself. "Not just booklovers, but parents looking for great gifts for their children, and those who want to connect with the history of this place. I can almost picture Beatrix Potter sitting in that corner, dreaming up Peter Rabbit."

"Oh, she didn't dream him up here but in Brompton Cemetery. That's where she got names for her characters. From the tombstones. Kinda like how you were named, in a roundabout way."

"I'm logging that detail about the cemetery." I pressed a finger to my temple. "What I'm trying to say is this place has so much charm and possibility—"

"What shop instilled your love of bookstores?"

"Uh, I'm not sure there was one."

"That's a shame. This one did it for me, but it would be highly unusual if it hadn't." She pointed to my tablet, the back of which was covered with stickers from different author homes I'd visited in New

England. "At least I know your passion for stories hasn't dimmed while slogging away at Triple B. Do you think you'll be able to keep your love of literature a year from now? Ten?"

This was the strangest business meeting I'd ever been involved in. Like I was being grilled by the world's sweetest person, but thoroughly raked over the coals, nonetheless.

"This is my personal tablet," I said, trying to explain its obviously unprofessional appearance. "My work laptop died before—"

"I think I prefer this one." Taking the tablet from me, she ran her finger over the Louisa May Alcott sticker. "I went to her house in Massachusetts once. I think that's something we have in common."

"Alcott or Massachusetts?" I asked, not sure how either applied.

"The love of history pertaining to authors," she replied, shooting me a look that said I was a bit dense, but she forgave me nonetheless. "This city lives and breathes writing. You're here how many days?"

"Three." My spirits sank at the number.

"That's not a lot of time."

I offered a *what can you* do shrug, though I'd been thinking the exact same thing. It was way too short, considering I wasn't meeting Glory until later tonight. It seemed like an eternity away.

"Do I get you the whole time?"

"Excuse me?" My heart pounded. Was she

suggesting that closing this deal could take three full days? "I had only counted on today. In fact, I have plans later tonight. I'd hoped to finish by six."

"I see." She tapped her chin with a finger. "As it happens, I, too, have a prior engagement this evening. Six o'clock, you say? I think I can work with that, but we better get a start on it."

"Great." I went to retrieve my tablet, but she hugged it closer to her chest.

"No. We're not wasting time on spreadsheets and charts."

I stared at her. "In that case, I have no idea what you expect of me."

"Nothing at all. The pressure is on me, not you. I have nine"—she pushed up her sleeve to consult her watch. "No, eight and a half hours to convince you London is so special for booklovers."

"I'm already a booklover. You don't need to convince me. It's the people out there that need convincing to come in here and buy books."

"No. I'm not worried about them." Cleo leaped to her feet. "But you, I want to prove to you that London isn't just a flag pushed into Triple B's plan to take over all the bookshops in the world. London can't be conquered. Believe me; many have tried."

"You make Triple B sound as bad as the Luftwaffe bombing raids in World War II," I argued, coming to my employer's defense. "I really don't think you have the right idea about us at all."

"I'm certain I do. Sheila? I'm heading out." After alerting her shop assistant that the completely empty store would soon be all hers to manage, Cleo glanced down at me, her face pink with excitement. "Why aren't you getting up? We don't have any time to waste."

I wasn't sure what she meant by *we*, but I certainly couldn't afford to dillydally, which was why I kept my keister planted firmly in the seat. No way was I going to let this woman whisk me out of the shop and derail me from inking this deal. My entire future at Triple B depended on this.

CHAPTER FIVE

"IT'S A TEMPTING OFFER," I told her flatly, "but I simply can't. My boss didn't send me over here to sightsee. I'm supposed to convince you to sign on the dotted line, along with a lot of initialing. The details are always in the initialing. If I don't, I'm out of a job."

I hadn't intended to be quite so transparent in my response, but it was probably better this way. Too many things were unexpected about Cleo Braithwaite, not least of which was the way her gaze seemed capable of penetrating my soul, leaving me defenseless and more than a little woozy. The sooner we got back to familiar footing, the better.

You have a date tonight, I reminded myself with more force than should have been necessary. *And Cleo Braithwaite isn't your friend.*

"This is only one shop." Cleo retook her seat with

a resounding thud. "They would honestly fire you for failing to close this deal?"

"Yes." Unable to stare into those penetrating eyes a moment longer, I glanced down at my favorite sticker, a raven for Poe's story. "But Braithwaite is a pretty big deal."

"Why do you want me to sign with a company that clearly has no morals?" Cleo spluttered.

"The truth is, I sort of stuck my neck out and promised I could get the job done, if only they'd agree to send me." *All because I wanted to meet a girl,* I added silently, kicking myself for my earlier bravado. "I'm surprised they picked me even if my email was full of exaggeration."

"That was partially my fault." She placed a hand on my arm, warm and comforting. The remorse was evident in her voice. "When the representative from Triple B approached me about this meeting, I insisted they send a woman. I understand you're the only one in the department."

"I don't want to lose my job." To my complete horror, my bottom lip started to quiver. I bit into it to make it stop. "They offer really good medical insurance. And dental. There's even talk of adding vision insurance."

She nodded, seeming to appreciate the gravity of the situation. "I'm even more convinced."

I let out a sigh of relief. "Great. Let me just—"

"Sightseeing is exactly what you need to perk you

up. London has a way of lifting even the most miserable souls. Like Ebenezer Scrooge."

Had she lost her marbles?

"I… can't… because… job…" Forget about the stiff upper lip thing the British seemed to admire so much. I was full-on blubbering. Like the really ugly type.

"Hey now." Cleo moved her chair closer and wrapped an arm around me. "Everything's going to be okay. I know right now you think the world is crashing down, but let me tell you, it only seems that way. The sun always comes out."

I couldn't speak because when I cried, getting words dislodged from my clogged throat was impossible. While I wanted to believe everything would be just dandy, I didn't see a way it would. How would I get another job that would pay enough to keep my apartment in New York? Moving home would be admitting defeat, not to mention getting me further away from Glory, which was the real dagger to the heart. I couldn't lose my job *and* move back to the Midwest. I had to find a way to convince this woman to look at my spreadsheets. They told the whole story!

Another sob escaped me.

"There, there." She patted my back.

A box of tissues appeared, either by magic or because Sheila, too, had noticed my distress and brought them over. I grabbed several sheets, crumpling and pressing them against my face to catch the overflow of tears. Cleo's arm rested across my back, her hand cupping my shoulder as if to hold me steady.

And then the strangest thing happened. I snuggled closer to this woman whom I didn't know, which was about the furthest possible thing from my normal personality. I wasn't really the type who liked being touched by strangers. Not only that, she was part of the reason why my world was crashing down around me. But I couldn't pull apart.

Come on, Marley.

Sniffling, I pulled myself upright, away from the comforting warmth of her arms. It was a long shot, but there was only one way forward I could see where I might still get what I wanted out of the day.

"Fine," I announced, putting back in place whatever was left of my professional veneer. "Let's go sightseeing."

CHAPTER SIX

"SPLENDID!" Cleo's eyes lit up like a child who'd just been promised a day at the circus, complete with cotton candy. "I want to show you why London is such a fabulous place for authors, in the past and now. While we're out and about, you can try to convince me to sign the deal. That way we can both get what we want out of the day."

"You want me to show you a PowerPoint presentation and spreadsheets while sightseeing?" I eyed my tablet, not seeing how that would work.

"No." Cleo shuddered. "To be clear, I never want you to show me a PowerPoint presentation or spreadsheets. *Spreadsheets*—it's got to be one of the worst words in history."

"But—"

"No buts. This isn't the day for negativity. It's a glorious London day. The sky is blue. The temperature is mild. And, there's so much to see. Your time is limited, and it's on me, as someone who loves this city, to share that with you."

"So, you lied to me, then. About listening to my pitch." I crossed my arms over my chest.

"I did not. I want you to talk to me. Not hide behind a device, showing me numbers, graphs, or whatever else was in your fancy presentation you've been so desperate to bore me with. You need to convince me, that you, Marley Royce, are right for the job. Do that, and I'll sign on the spot."

She wanted me to sweet-talk her. I could do that if I dug deep. On a business level, that was. Strictly business. Having reminded myself of that part, I found I needed to drag my eyes up to hers. They'd mischievously wandered to the neckline of the peasant blouse she was wearing.

Let me just say that outfit didn't do any justice to the curves hidden beneath it, which I'd had the chance to experience as she'd held me while I sobbed like a baby. But that was neither here nor there. I was here on business, and business is what I intended to conduct. Even if I had to do it from the top of a double-decker tour bus.

"I'm in town for seventy-two hours," I said. "I guess I have that long to convince you." The way things were looking, I'd be lucky to cram in a coffee with Glory.

"Non-stop?"

"Well, no," I corrected, tripping over my words. It had to have been my overactive imagination, but I could have sworn she waggled her eyebrows in what could only be described as a suggestive manner. "We'll have to sleep. Separately. Er...uh... Sleep is important."

What the hell was wrong with me? One—probably imaginary—eyebrow waggle and apparently my subconscious had plummeted straight to the gutter. Under different circumstances, flirting with a smart and attractive woman like Cleo would have been the highlight of my day, but she was a client. And I already had a date for later that night. Why did I have to keep reminding myself of that when it was the whole reason I was here?

Keep it professional, Marley.

"I do enjoy sleeping," Cleo commented, seemingly unaware of my inner turmoil. "I get nine and a half hours every night."

I burst into laughter but then realized she was absolutely serious. "How do you manage that? By the time I get home from the office, fix myself dinner, and get ready for bed, I'm lucky if I have even eight hours before I have to get up and do it all over again."

"You Americans." She shook her head, her demeanor more one of sympathy than judgement. "If there's one thing I'd like you to learn while you're in London, it's that working yourself to death isn't the only way to live."

"I like to eat and have a roof over my head, though," I explained. "Working makes that possible for me. That is, unless I lose this account. Then I won't have either. I think you're missing that part."

"I'm not. You can dazzle me with your business acumen while I dazzle you with my favorite city destinations. But there's one thing you need to know about me. I don't believe one should ever compromise on the quality of life. Repeat after me: no compromising."

"You just did," I pointed out, even though part of me knew it was wiser to keep my mouth shut since I was getting my way. "You compromised by agreeing to listen to my spiel."

"I said not to compromise on the quality of your life." She gave me a look that was part amusement and part exasperation. "We can sit in this room all day splitting hairs, but that's not your best bet to winning me over."

"It's your business I'm trying to win," I said, splitting hairs again. But given all the improper places my brain kept wandering, I felt it was necessary to reiterate.

"I know as a small business owner this might be scandalous for me to admit, but I hate the business side of life. I prefer living. So, let's get outside and do just that, shall we?"

Damn it if her enthusiasm didn't crack my wall. I did want to see London. I'd wanted to ever since I heard my first Dickens story as a child. Now, I was in the country with a descendent of one of the oldest booksellers in England. One of Cleo's relatives probably knew Charles Dickens personally. How could I say no?

CHAPTER SEVEN

"I NEED to use the little girls' room before we go," I said.

"The what?" Cleo appeared perplexed. "I'm afraid the shop doesn't have any special area for children."

I ran through what I'd said, realized my error, and tried again. "Your restroom?"

"We really don't have time for you to take a nap before we go. We're short on time as it is."

"No." I waved my hands in front of me as if to erase everything. "I need to use the bathroom."

"I would have thought you'd have bathed before coming here," Cleo said, but this time, her wicked smirk clued me in she was teasing. "If it's the toilet you're looking for, it's through that door next to where Sheila is stocking the graphic novels."

I chuckled to myself as I walked in the direction Cleo had pointed. Some people might have been annoyed by that style of teasing, but I found it charming. Maybe it was the accent.

Once I was inside the bathroom—and I refuse to say I was inside the toilet because it makes it sound like I was taking a swim—I paused for a moment to attend to the most pressing matter, which was to send a message to Glory.

Made it to my business meeting on time.

Was she as scary as you feared?

I grinned as I recalled the long conversations we'd had about this leading up to my trip. Some of the research I'd found online about Cleo Braithwaite had been enough to give me nightmares. If only I'd known all along that was her mother and not her, I wouldn't have nearly given myself an ulcer over it.

Not at all, I admitted. *She actually seems nice.*

I told you not to worry.

You were right, I replied.

It wasn't much of a revelation. In the time I'd known Glory, she usually was. I took an extra second to look at her tiny avatar before putting the phone back in my bag.

"Ready?" Cleo asked when I rejoined her in the shop a few minutes later. "Everything okay?"

"Fine," I assured her but then rethought my reply as I glanced down at my carefully chosen suit and shiny high-heeled shoes. It was perfect for a day of presentations, but not so great for sightseeing. "Actually, is there room in your schedule for us to stop at my hotel so I can change clothes?"

Her eyes traveled the length of me, causing my skin to tingle in a strange and delightful way. Given there was nothing inappropriate in how she was looking at me, my physical reaction was outrageously over-the-top. I prayed it didn't show on my face.

"Where is your hotel?" When she heard the name, she appeared to know exactly where it was. "We'll go right past it on our way to the Tube."

My room was ready when I arrived at the front desk, and they'd even been kind enough to bring up the bag I'd left, boosting my belief that all those British good manners I'd heard about weren't merely a myth.

"Shall I wait down here?" Cleo asked as the clerk handed me my key.

"Unless you'd like to come up."

"A scandalous invitation, considering we've only just met." That time, there was no denying the shake of the eyebrow. It was clear as day and could only mean one thing.

Cleo Braithwaite was flirting with me.

"I… uh…"

"Relax." She winked, and I felt the now-familiar tingling sensation travel at lightning speed all the way to the tip of my toes. "I promise not to breathe a word of your indecent proposal to the Triple B corporate office."

I stumbled my way to the elevator and had barely regained my balance by the time I made it to my room. As promised, my suitcase was waiting, and when I unzipped it, the first thing I found was my little black dress and fancy underwear. I stared at them dumbly, trying to remember why they were there. Was I supposed to put them on now?

It's for your date tonight, stupid.

How could I have forgotten, even for a second? Something was seriously off-kilter with me. Taking extra effort to focus, I stripped off my work clothes and put on a comfortable pair of worn jeans, a button-up plaid shirt, and a soft cardigan. Finally, I slipped on thick socks and walking shoes, my toes wiggling with delight at all the extra room they'd lucked into.

As I exited my room, I cast a final glance at my date night ensemble that I'd put on the bed to change into when I returned. I tried to picture myself wearing it beside a life-sized version of Glory's avatar but failed. I regretted for at least the millionth time agreeing not to exchange photos. That it might make it easier to resist Cleo's charms was a fact I didn't want to contemplate too closely.

Once I returned to the lobby, Cleo was eager to usher me back onto the street and into the nearest Tube station. Minutes later, we resurfaced at the Westminster stop, spilling out onto the sidewalk, smashing into a rush of people.

Cleo took my hand, glancing over her shoulder, saying, "Follow me!"

She was like a valiant knight trying to save me, the poor American damsel in distress, as I walked on the wrong side of the sidewalk and met with resistance at every step.

Honestly, I'd been living in New York long enough to navigate my way through crowds, but I didn't mind Cleo holding my hand. Purely from a practical standpoint. Given I didn't know our destination, I couldn't lead, now could I?

In fact, I was about to ask her where we were headed when—wait, was that Big Ben?

Not watching my step, I rammed right into Cleo.

"Sorry. I got distracted." The next thing I knew, I was rooted in place, staring deeply into her eyes.

"That happens a lot in London." She made no effort to look away.

Seconds ticked by. My heart started to race or possibly stopped beating entirely. I'm not exactly sure which. I didn't even know if this woman was gay for certain, but what had seemed like flirting back in the hotel took on a different quality here, an almost cosmic connection.

Or maybe I only thought that because she was dressed like a carnival tent palm reader.

"Um, is that Big Ben?" I pointed to the iconic clock tower.

"Nope," she informed me without so much as cracking a smile. "That one is Little Ben."

I turned to her, my mouth agape. "There are two of them?"

"No!" Now, she laughed, pointing at my face. "I love that look you get when you're trying to determine if I'm fucking with you or not."

"Are you?"

Her devilish smile was doing things to me. Pleasant but also torturous things. This innocent sightseeing trip threatened all sorts of unexpected turns that could have been thrilling, if only I didn't have a date waiting for me later today.

"Depends who you ask," she answered right before the pause between us became awkward.

"I'm asking you."

This caused a slight flutter of her eyelids, but I was certain it wasn't because I'd upset her. The opposite really. "A bold approach. So many prefer to hear secondhand what other people think is going through my head."

"I'm not big on gossip. Besides"—I hefted a shoulder—"I don't know anyone here except you."

"No? I thought you said you had plans tonight. Or were you trying to pressure me into a quick sale by pretending?"

"No, nothing like that. It's a little—" I was about to say *complicated* when I was interrupted by the sonorous tolling of a bell. It played a little song, followed by a deep gong and then nine more. "It's ten o'clock. I can't believe I'm listening to the actual Big Ben. I could do this all day."

"I think you'd be disappointed. The next couple of hours might be enjoyable, but once it strikes twelve, it's all downhill. Besides, this isn't our destination."

"It isn't?" I'd been certain Cleo had timed the whole thing to perfection for me.

"No, but it's impossible to go from one place to the next in this city without getting distracted by something marvelous."

After one final glance at the famous clock, I motioned for her to lead the way. The crowds weren't as thick here, so she didn't reach for my hand as she had before. I was oddly disappointed, missing the touch.

CHAPTER EIGHT

"THAT'S WESTMINSTER ABBEY!" I gawked at the gothic cathedral, unable to think of anything else to say, except *OMG*, but that would've made me sound like a teenager. I'd begun to suspect Cleo was much more sophisticated in the ways of business than she let on, or that I'd at first assumed, and coming across as a slack-jawed yokel would hardly earn me her trust or get that coveted signature on the dotted line.

Whipping my phone out of my bag, I prepared to snap a photo. Cleo ducked into the shot at the last second, a wild expression on her face, and I tucked my phone away. Had I really just used the word sophisticated to describe her? I held back a snort. Truthfully, though, she managed to be playful and savvy at the same time, which was an alarmingly intoxicating combination.

"I'm sorry. I didn't mean to spoil your photo." Cleo's tone was contrite.

"Not at all," I said with a laugh. I pulled the phone back out and showed her the shot with a grin. "It's perfect, see? I simply wanted to take in the impressive architecture from here on out and not hide behind my phone."

"Very wise. I'm amazed by how many tourists spend their entire holiday staring at a screen, taking photos and video instead of living in the moment." Cleo pointed to a line of people. "We should join the queue. Luckily, it's November. I never come here in July or August. Way too many people."

She plugged her nose as a way to show her displeasure with them, or so I assumed. It wasn't likely she was implying everyone was stinkier during the summer months. Although, that could also be true. The New York subway in the hot and humid months always had a more pungent stench, and I doubted London, for all its magic, was any better.

We got behind a couple who were waiting at the back of the line. As the woman chattered with great enthusiasm, the dude stared at his phone, offering only the occasional grunt in return.

Cleo rolled her eyes at this living example of our previous conversation, and I quietly snickered.

"Are we going to Poets' Corner?" I asked, keeping my cool as best I could. The truth was, I could barely contain myself from jumping up and down, begging for her to say yes.

"Damn." She snapped her fingers in an exaggerated way. "I was hoping to surprise you. It's ruined now. I guess we should just skip—"

"Uh-uh!" I tugged on her arm. "Not a chance."

"For someone who didn't want to leave the shop today, you've drastically changed your tune."

"What? Oh, that... yes." My heart plunged to my toes. For a few seconds there, I'd forgotten about work. "I suppose we should head back—"

"I wouldn't dream of it. It's not every day a woman named Marley gets to pay respects to her literary... *godfather*?" The final word came out as a question, like she wasn't certain if that was the right term, but I instantly loved it.

"That's the perfect way to describe him, isn't it?" I'd have to break my no camera policy because my dad would kill me if I didn't take a selfie next to Dickens's tombstone. "If you'd explained that this was the plan, I may not have resisted so much."

"And take the fun out of seeing your eyes light up when you spied Big Ben and then the Abbey?"

"I've always wanted to come here," I confided, still hardly able to believe this was real. "In college, I dated a woman named Abby, and she hated the fact that I always misspelled her name, adding the E before the Y."

"I also dated an Abby once upon a time, but she wasn't nearly so unreasonable about spelling."

Bingo! I came about half a second away from yelling this out like I was in a church basement and expecting to win a prize. Luckily, I realized how bad that would make me look and kept it inside. Unless Abby was a boy name in Britain, which I highly doubted, Cleo dug chicks, which dramatically increased the odds she'd been flirting with me earlier.

"Do you know when Poets' Corner got its start?" she asked without a hint of strangeness, making me very grateful she only dressed like a psychic and couldn't actually read my mind.

I was still too busy patting myself on the back for my exceptional gaydar and couldn't pull that bit of literary trivia from my brain, so I shook my head.

"Back in 1400, Geoffrey Chaucer, who penned *The Canterbury Tales,* as you probably already know—was the first poet to be buried here. However, it was because he'd been the Clerk of the King's Works and had been in charge of the repairs of the Abbey, not because he was a poet."

"1400? I think the oldest church in America is in Santa Fe, New Mexico, and it dates back to the 1600s, if memory serves. I was there this summer. It's adobe, though, not—" I tilted my head back to take in the splendor in front of me, mouthing *wow*.

"Are you a church aficionado?" Cleo arched an eyebrow, like she was trying to figure me out.

"Not for religious purposes, but I find churches fascinating."

"Too bad we can't go to St. Paul's," she said somewhat mournfully.

"Why can't we?" I fixed her with my best impression of a puppy being deprived of a piece of pepperoni.

She burst out laughing. "Maybe I can work it into the schedule somewhere. I don't want sadness to infiltrate those eyes ever again."

"What do you mean?" I doubled down on my canine impersonation, adding a slight whimper and tilt of my head.

"Okay," she said like a little kid calling out *uncle* to stop the torment. "You're a very hard woman to resist, Marley Royce."

Her words sent a flush of excitement through me I thought best not to analyze.

CHAPTER NINE

I STARED down at the memorial embedded in the stone floor. *"Near this stone lie buried..."* I murmured, saying the words out loud. The first name was Geoffrey Chaucer. "If he was buried here because of his duties, how did Poets' Corner become—" I waved to the stones and monuments that surrounded us, searching for a word to do it justice and coming up empty. I had an audio guide, but I found I didn't need to listen since Cleo was a fountain of knowledge and would share on demand without so much as pressing a button.

"Do you know Edmund Spenser?" she asked.

I shook my head, not wanting to bluff. She would know and test me for sure. I barely knew her, but I had little doubt Cleo was the type to put one on the spot. She knew her stuff, too. It was possible she knew even

49

more about history and literature than Glory did, a feat I hadn't thought possible.

"He wrote *The Faerie Queene*, which he dedicated to Elizabeth the First, and he requested being buried next to Chaucer. That began this tradition of memorials and burials for poets and writers. Happily, it's a tradition that continues to this day. In 2013, C.S. Lewis got a stone on the fiftieth anniversary of his death." She waved to a different stone. "He's the first writer from Belfast to be included here."

"I love his books. Oh, look. Here's D.H. Lawrence, Lewis Carroll, and Henry James." A rush coursed through me. "I can't believe I'm standing here." I closed my eyes, placing my hands over my heart. "It's like I'm being blessed with their literary greatness."

She quietly chuckled. "I still get goose bumps, and I can't remember all the times I've come. Like you, I'm not religious, but if I were, this would be where I'd come to worship."

"Is Shakespeare here?" Just the thought made the hair on my arms stand at attention, and I raised one to show Cleo. "Look at this. You must think I'm crazy."

"Not at all. It's the sign of a true booklover. But to answer your question, no. Shakespeare isn't here, not his remains at least. However, there's a statue of him." She pointed at a marble statue that was life-size. Standing with one leg crossing the other, he leaned on three books stacked on a pediment.

I savored the moment.

"If you had to choose between only reading Shake-speare or Dickens, which would it be?" She gazed at me with intense curiosity.

"Why are you being cruel?" I pouted. "That's like asking someone to pick a favorite child or only one dessert."

"Sorry, but that's the rule." She waved for me to name my poison, so to speak.

"Dickens, naturally," I said, though my tone made it clear I wasn't happy about it. "How could I not, given my name?"

Cleo took my arm again, leading me onto the floor. I stiffened at first, having the sense of walking across people's graves. But others were doing the same, so I followed. She stopped and pointed to a simple marker. It read *Charles Dickens* and was carved with his birth and death dates.

"Is that all?" I scrunched my brow. "He's a legend. His books are the reason I loved London before ever stepping foot on the plane."

"It was his wish to keep it simple. He actually stip-ulated in his will that his name be memorialized this way. His grave was dug at night, and only a dozen people attended the burial."

"That's all? Surely the public wanted to come, too."

"The grave was left open, and soon enough, the papers got the word out." Cleo's eyes misted, and a half-smile settled on her lips, almost as though she could picture the scene in her mind. "Thousands of people came to pay their respects, tossing in flowers. It was closed two or three days later. Every year, on the anniversary of his death, a wreath is laid upon his grave."

"I have to admit that kinda surprises me. Nell's death scene was so sentimental..." I let my voice trail off.

"Whatever else Mr. Dickens may have been, he was thoroughly British."

"What does that mean?"

"We don't like to make a fuss. Growing up, I recall the oft-told story of Captain Oates, who was part of the Terra Nova expedition to the South Pole in the early 1900s. They were beset by troubles, and Oates became ill and developed gangrene. He realized that by having to care for him, the others' lives were at risk. When they refused to leave him behind to better their chances of survival, he got up in the middle of a blizzard and said, *I'm just going outside, and I may be some time.*"

"Then what?"

"Presumably he died because he never returned."

"Wow," I mouthed, cognizant of the crowd around us, and looked back to Charles Dickens's simple stone.

"The quintessential English gentleman, Oates was. All of them, really. They brought a silver pot with them to serve tea."

"Did the others make it?" I asked.

"Sadly, no. They all froze to death in the end."

"Maybe they should have brought more blankets instead of fancy teapots," I muttered.

Cleo arched an eyebrow. "Come, now. We wouldn't want to be savages."

"No wonder you don't like Americans."

She slanted her head. "Why do you think that?"

"You've made it clear you hate Triple B. You haven't come out and said it in those exact terms, but I can see it in your eyes whenever the company is mentioned. Yep, it's right there." I pointed with my finger.

"I don't hate all Americans across the board. I actually enjoy American earnestness and can-do spirit. Don't read into my dislike of your company as me disliking you. That's not true at all."

I found myself drawn in by this admission, curious to figure out what it entailed.

CHAPTER TEN

WHEN WE FINALLY DEPARTED WESTMINSTER ABBEY SOME thirty minutes later and stepped back outside into the sunshine, it was so much brighter in comparison that I needed to pull out my sunglasses. By my count, this was the fourth weather change of the day, and it was only midmorning.

"What's next?" I asked.

"I have a stop in mind, but it's a bit of a walk along the river. Thirty minutes. Is that okay?"

"Yes because strolling along the Thames is *such* a hardship," I teased.

"Complete torture." She flashed me a smile. "I'm glad we're in agreement, because I can't think of a more glorious way to soak in some rays."

We arrived at the Westminster Bridge, and I noticed people walking on the sides. It wasn't the first time I'd walked across a bridge, but this was the first time I crossed the Thames.

"Did you know the bridge is painted the same shade of green as the leather seats in the House of Commons?" Cleo asked.

I shook my head, amused by how much she seemed to enjoy sharing these tidbits with me. For my part, I was enthralled, not to mention beyond impressed at her unending supply of trivia.

When we were halfway across the bridge, I stopped to take in the sight of the river flowing underneath us. "I can't believe I'm standing here."

"It's a beautiful sight, isn't it?" She peered down with an expression of genuine admiration, despite certainly having seen it thousands of times before. It lifted my heart to know my tour guide was getting as much out of the day as I was, despite how strange it still seemed that we were exploring the city when we were supposed to be working.

A red speed boat zipped past on the water. Another, much larger boat that was filled with tourists plodded along at a slower speed. Both just seemed so wrong. In my mind, I could picture the Thames filled instead with majestic sailing ships as it had been for much of its history. Although, who could blame people for wanting to see the sights from the water? Secretly, I wished we could, but time was limited.

Continuing on, we reached the south side of the river.

"Are you sad we're not discussing business?" Cleo's voice was teasing as she nudged me with her elbow.

"In the moment, no. When I lose my job when I get back, perhaps." I spied the London Eye, unable to suppress a grin despite the dread churning inside me.

"You're not going to lose your job." She said this with such confidence I didn't want to argue the point, even though it was clear she'd never worked for a corporation like Triple B. Here we were, walking along the Thames and having a marvelous day, and my job seemed so far away that losing it hardly seemed to matter. Or, I tried telling myself that.

A mother pulled the handle of a scooter, a small child standing on it, along for the ride.

"That's a brilliant way to get kids from point A to point B." I looked over my shoulder. The little girl waved and smiled at me. I did the same.

"Do you want kids?" Cleo's sudden inquiry nearly stopped me in my tracks. Though I could draw a line from point A to point B and see how she'd come to ask it, I still found it jarring. Even so, instead of closing up as I might've done when things became too personal, I found myself giving my answer serious consideration.

"I haven't given it much thought before," I admitted. "Maybe I should now that I'm nearing thirty-five, but every time I try to see myself with kids, or even my future, I can't really picture it in my head. It's more like a contemporary art piece, splotches here and there of color but no discernible images."

I worried my answer made me sound immature, but Cleo's eyes held no judgment. Instead, she smiled warmly, her eyes crinkling. "That's the loveliest description of life I've ever heard."

"Is it? Truth be told, it kinda scares me. I'm nearing forty, and what do I have to show for it?"

"You just said you were nearing thirty-five, and now it's forty," Cleo pointed out. "How old are you, exactly?"

"I turned thirty-three last month."

Cleo let out a whoop of laughter. "You've got the better part of your thirties ahead of you before you need to start worrying about what you have to show for it."

"It doesn't feel that way," I argued. "Compared to the people around me, I'm way behind. I'm not in a relationship. I thought living in New York would be all restaurants and Broadway shows, but it's a struggle to make enough money to keep a roof over my head and food in my fridge. Sometimes I wonder what's the point to everything."

"And your job?"

I gave a noncommittal shrug, which admittedly wasn't the strongest response considering I was supposed to be convincing her to sign with my company, but it was hard to lie to her.

"Why work so hard when you can barely afford anything or stop and"—she waved her arm to the water—"enjoy the view? Maybe this trip will turn out to be just what you need."

"How so?"

"I've found when at a crossroads, which it seems you might be right now, clearing one's mind with a stroll through London puts everything into perspective." She plucked at my sleeve, encouraging me to start walking again. "But don't lose sight of that vision in your head. All the splotches of color. To me, that's the beauty of life. Enjoying the way sunlight glimmers on the surface of the river or how spring flowers look after a cleansing rain."

"When I get old, I don't want to have regrets." My lack of hesitation confiding in this woman surprised me, but it did feel better to get my thoughts out in the open. She was so easy to talk to, and her obvious intelligence gave her opinions extra weight.

"You must enjoy anything and everything you see. Don't take things for granted." Cleo smiled, not seeming to think it strange at all that she was having this conversation with someone she'd only recently met. "This, my dear Marley, is the definition of a life well lived. I'm well aware how bloody fortunate I am to have grown up in this city. I can't think of another place I'd like to be. Yes, I enjoy traveling, but coming home to London, it's the greatest gift."

"That's just it. I don't feel that way when I return to New York after a business trip."

"What do you feel?" She stopped and gazed at me with an intensity that I could feel in my bones.

"Sadness."

"Sounds to me like you're not in the right place."

I sighed. "Perhaps not, but I don't see any way to make a change. I wish—"

"Wish what?"

"Never mind." I shook my head. I'd been about to say I wished I was as brave as her, that I could see life the way she did. But what kind of thing was that to say to someone I'd only just met?

CHAPTER ELEVEN

I STOOD outside a brick building with red-painted window trim and doors, digging out my phone. No unread texts, I noted, though it wasn't too much of a surprise. Glory had a full day of work to pay attention to, just as I did. Or, at least, as I was supposed to.

Counting the hours until tonight, I messaged, experiencing a hint of guilt at the fact I was playing hooky at a pub instead of slogging through my presentation in a stuffy conference room. With a beautiful woman, no less. This day wasn't playing out at all the way I'd thought it would, and I was conflicted over how to feel about it.

I tucked my phone into my bag as Cleo came out of the building with two miniature drinks in hand. Introspection would have to wait on the back burner for another time.

"Here ya go!" Handing me one glass, she lifted her

own as if to give a toast. "It's a little indulgent to be drinking before lunch, but we couldn't very well stop and not partake, at least a little."

I held the tiny glass at eye-level, grinning. "This is brilliant."

"The lager?" She didn't sound convinced. She simultaneously boosted one eyebrow, reinforcing her skepticism.

"No, the glass," I explained. "It's so small."

"It's a half-pint." Cleo took a sip, managing to look ever so dainty, like a baby hedgehog drinking from a thimble.

"Is this their special gimmick?" I studied the pub's name, The Anchor, not making an obvious connection to Hobbit-sized beers.

"No, it's a standard pub thing. They all do it."

"Why don't we have this in the US?" I asked with envy. "In America, we only go bigger, not smaller."

"I have noticed that about your compatriots."

"So—" I flourished my glass at the pub. "Since we walked past The Globe on our way here, I must ask. Did William Shakespeare partake here?"

"I don't think so. This pub opened in 1616, the same year Shakespeare died, but he wasn't in London at that point. He'd retired to Stratford-upon-Avon by then."

"Where he was born in 1564," I added, eager to demonstrate my own knowledge of literary trivia.

Cleo nodded, seeming impressed. "That's right."

"Wait?" I eyed the brick building again. "How old is this pub?"

"Four hundred years, give or take." She arched that eyebrow again, making my pulse quicken. It was a skill I'd always wanted and could never master, but I'd be lying if I said I wasn't a sucker for women who could.

"That's just so hard to wrap my brain around. Yes, I realize I was the one who asked if Shakespeare drank here, but it wasn't until you mentioned the actual years, nudging my brain that we're in the twenty-first century now. Wow. Four hundred years." I flicked my fingers out on either side of my ears, miming my head exploding. "America isn't even two-hundred and fifty years old yet." I started laughing.

Cleo looked at me with a quizzical expression. "What's so funny?"

"This pub is older than my country."

She smiled indulgently, seeming to be taken by my incredulity over a fact most Britons not only knew but understood in the core of their being. How could they not? The physical proof of how old their institutions were was everywhere around them, even in a common pub.

"Did any famous people drink here?" I asked when I'd gotten over my shock. "Back in the old days?"

"Oh, yes." Cleo's eyes twinkled with that look I was starting to recognize as the one that said she had a story to tell, and I found myself holding my breath in anticipation. "This pub has an interesting history, really. It's one of the remaining riverside inns that were around during the height of the theaters here, including the Globe. In 1666, Samuel Pepys was here, during the Great Fire of London on the other side of the river."

"The diarist?"

"The very one." Her expression said she was impressed, as not everyone would have gotten the reference. I flushed with pride. "He jotted down that he'd taken sanctuary in an alehouse and watched the fire grow."

I glanced toward the structures on the far side of the river, trying to imagine what that must have been like to observe firsthand.

"This pub was also frequented by smugglers and pirates," she continued. "During one of the times it was being repaired, they discovered secret places, which more than likely were used to conceal contraband."

"Pirates," I breathed. Again, my eyes wandered back to the water, trying to conjure up ships conveying stolen goods. "It's fun to think about, isn't it? All the things these bricks have been privy to over the centuries."

"I've spent many lazy afternoons sitting in a pub, envisioning certain stories."

"*Treasure Island* was one of the first books I read on my own when I was a kid." I took a swallow of beer, warmed as much by it as by the kinship I felt with this fellow booklover. "For the next three years on Halloween, I dressed as a pirate."

"Do you remember the first book you read?"

"Who can forget their first?" My words came out more provocatively than I'd intended, which didn't go unnoticed given what was becoming her trademark boosted eyebrow, which did things to me I didn't know possible by such a simple act. My cheeks went from their former light flush to a burning scarlet.

"Do tell." The blatant seduction in her tone upped the ante.

"*Little House in the Big Woods.*" I burst out laughing, realizing how very not sexy that answer was.

"*The Wind in the Willows.*" She patted her chest, drawing my attention to her attributes once again and sparking a rush of feelings that weren't at all appropriate for the discussion of children's books.

"Another classic." I looked back to the water, which seemed like the safest option because her eyes were bewitching and her cleavage a temptation. What the hell was wrong with me? I patted the pocket where I'd placed my phone, wishing Glory would text, if only to remind me I needed to behave. I was spoken for, sort of.

"I've always found it fascinating that American and British children's literature are so different."

"How do you mean?"

"A lot of your stories are grounded in morality. Like Huck Finn, getting on a raft to right a social wrong.

While many of our stories are fantastical. I think part of it goes back to our origin story, King Arthur learning from a wizard. Your history is grounded in the Protestant work ethic." She shook a fist in the air, which I assumed was directed at work in general and Puritans in particular. After all, it had been her idea not to work today.

I took another drink of beer, mulling that over. "I've never really looked at it that way."

"It's easier to see things from a distance. I didn't really start to make the connections until I traveled through America. I was always amazed by the can-do spirit of many whom I met along the way."

"Is that not a thing here?"

"Oh, we have overachievers, but the difference is we won't admit it. Most of us go out of our way to say we're average, even when the evidence stacks up against us." Her eyes were on the water, as if I should let this go.

Yeah, right. That was not going to happen.

CHAPTER TWELVE

"I TAKE it you're above average, then." I took a sip of my beer, watching Cleo squirm.

"Of course not," she protested. "I'm perfectly average."

"I highly doubt that. You're a walking encyclopedia of London history, and you quote the classics at the drop of a hat. I don't believe for a minute that anyone would consider you average."

"Shh. People will hear." She placed a finger to her lips and started laughing. "What about you?"

"Sadly, I really am very average," I admitted. "Growing up, I never had grand ambitions like becoming a doctor or a lawyer. I just wanted to be surrounded by books."

"Which makes you far from average," Cleo pointed out.

"If you're using it as a synonym for normal, I can't

argue. I'm the weirdo who stands in line at the post office, with my nose in a book. Sometimes"—I leaned closer to whisper my confession, and my nose was tickled by a delightful whiff of her musky scent—"I'm sad when there isn't a line because that means no reading time. Especially when I had to go to the post office for work."

"Triple B sends you to the post? I would have thought the company would have a mail room."

"Oh, this was a different job, when I was still in college. I was an author's assistant."

"That sounds thrilling," she said without a trace of sarcasm.

I laughed at the way her eyes glistened with excitement. "It wasn't as glamorous as it sounds, but it helped pay the bills and gave me that all-important real-world experience to put on my resumé."

"Have you always worked with books in some fashion?"

"Yep. My other college part-time job was at Borders, which was a bookstore that's long since gone out of business." I took a long swallow of beer, suddenly uncomfortable as I recalled that she, too, owned a bookstore that was teetering on the edge of collapse. "The problem with that job was the people."

"But the people are what make it worthwhile," Cleo argued. "Introducing readers to new books is one of the best parts of what I do."

"Maybe so, but the customers who came into our

store were obsessed with their coupons. It was funny because it was in a really wealthy neighborhood, but people would insist we ring up every transaction separately so they could reuse their ten-percent-off discount."

"That was allowed?" Cleo's lips pursed, her shrewd businesswoman persona clearly winning out over the magical book fairy part of her.

"Not once the corporate office figured out they were going bust and had to do everything to stop the hemorrhaging. That was a bad week." I grimaced at the memory. "Of course, it was the sales staff who got stuck delivering the bad news. When I had told our regulars they could only use the coupon once per visit... well, let's just say they weren't very polite. It was around that time I opted to work in the back room."

"Doing the bookkeeping?"

"Nothing that fancy. I'd arrive at six in the morning to unpack the books that had been delivered overnight. We'd sort them onto different carts—like for history, romance, business—and when the carts were full, we'd wheel them out to shelve the books. It was fantastic because we got four solid hours without a single customer. I also got to see and hold all of the new books coming in." I closed my eyes momentarily to relive the thrill. "I really miss that part. I work for a large chain, but I never get to handle the books anymore. It's like... what's the point to my job?"

Cleo cocked her head to the right, studying me. It made me nervous, like I'd said too much. I was supposed to be selling her on the idea of joining Triple B, and here I was bashing my job. I was the worst salesperson in the world. We had yet to discuss business, and at the rate I was going, she'd be completely scared off before I even started my proposal. Then I'd get fired for sure.

I downed my drink in one long gulp, regretting it instantly as my vision blurred around the edges.

"I think I might need lunch soon. This is going straight to my head." I hooked my thumb over my shoulder at the pub. "Do they serve food?"

"They do, but I have a better idea. As long as you're okay to walk a bit, that is."

"I'm not that bad." I held up my miniature glass. "It was only half a pint, after all. Also, I wouldn't mind another one of these today, if you can squeeze it onto our agenda."

"We're in London. Half-pints are *always* on the agenda. That's the best part of pub hopping and only indulging in halves. It takes four pubs to drink two beers." She set her glass on the ground next to the door of the pub but made no move to go inside. I eyed several other glasses that had been left in a similar fashion.

"You leave them there? It feels so rude."

"Here I thought we English were the polite ones."

Cleo chortled. "But, yes. It's the way things have always been."

"I can't do it. I'm not a fan of clutter or broken glass in my feet." I picked up Cleo's glass and a few others along with mine. "I'll be right back."

CHAPTER THIRTEEN

WE STARTED WALKING along the Thames again, and my vision bounced all over the place, not only because of the half-pint I'd drunk on an empty stomach. I wasn't quite as much of a lightweight as that. No, I was simply taking in as much as possible and trying to do it on both sides of the river at once. It was difficult and made my head spin, but that didn't stop me from trying.

"What are you doing?" Cleo asked when I stumbled into her, after weaving back and forth precariously more times than I wanted to admit. "Do I need to call for assistance?"

"I'm fine," I assured her, though I was pretty sure she'd been joking. "I never expected the river to be so wide."

"Yes, well, try not to fall into it."

I pursed my lips, preparing a smart comeback but

discovering I was fresh out. She had a point. I'd been steady as a drunken sailor. "Now I understand why pirates used the pub to hide their booty. Massive ships could come through here. Were there this many bridges back then?"

Glancing over my left shoulder, I spied one bridge, and up ahead of us was another.

"Now, for that question, I'll have to do some research. I'm not awfully familiar with pirates, but I do know when they built Tower Bridge, back in the late 1800s, there were still quite a few cargo ships coming and going. These days, it's mostly tourist boats. Back then, the ships would come in past Tower Bridge and unload into warehouses."

"If it's only smaller tourist boats, does that mean they don't raise the bridge anymore?" The sound of seagulls pierced the air, and I wished I could close my eyes to picture what it would have looked like back in the days of cargo ships and pirates, but I had taken Cleo's warning about not falling into the river to heart and didn't want to risk it despite the barrier. Let's face it. This day wasn't going as planned, so splashing into the water didn't seem so far-fetched.

"No, they still raise the bridge. In the old days, someone would keep a lookout for a ship. The difference now is permission to pass through has to be requested in writing twenty-four hours ahead of time."

"I'd love to see that!"

"Would you now?" There was a searching quality

to her question I couldn't entirely figure out.

"Absolutely." After I replied, it occurred to me she may have taken my comment to mean I wanted her to show this to me. It wasn't what I'd intended, but I also wouldn't say no if she asked. I decided not to clarify one way or another what I'd meant. "I know you have book connections, but the real question is, do you have any bridge ones?"

"I guess you'll never know," she said with a laugh. "You've only given me today, after all, to show you the sights. Unless, of course, you weren't joking about using all seventy-two hours to convince me to join the company you so clearly despise."

"You're the one who seems to hate my job," I argued. "Or my company, anyway. And I have no idea why."

She studied my face for a moment. "Do you really want to know?"

"I'm not sure." I glanced back to the river, suddenly nervous. Another tourist boat came into view. "Maybe it would be better if you let me do my job, convince you that whatever you've been led to believe about Triple B is clearly wrong."

"It's—" She stopped at that, and I couldn't figure out why, but I didn't have time to play her hesitancy over in my mind because suddenly something wondrous had come into view, removing all trace of work from my mind.

"What's that?" I extended my arm.

CHAPTER FOURTEEN

SHE FOLLOWED MY ARM, squinting. "Oh. That's the Golden Hinde."

"Is that where we're going next? We've only been walking a handful of minutes, and there's already another goody to admire." I spoke breathlessly as I took in the fully rigged tall ship nestled incongruously between buildings. For a moment, I wondered if it had traveled through time. If it had, the pirates onboard would be very surprised when they saw their surroundings.

"It's not officially on the agenda," Cleo told me with a sparkle in her eyes. "But given the bounce in your step, let's add it."

"Wait a minute. Are you saying you walk by shit like this every day, and it's like, *Oh, yeah, I totally forgot about this spectacular ship?*"

"Truthfully, yes." Cleo gave a shrug, driving home

exactly how commonplace this was for her. "Mind you this is one of many reasons I'll never leave London. I've lived here my entire life, and I'm still discovering more things to love."

"What's not to love about a city with pirate ships around every corner."

"Exactly, although whether or not Sir Francis Drake was a pirate depends on who you ask."

"This was Sir Francis Drake's ship?" I asked in awe.

"A replica, yes. His was the first English ship to sail around the world."

"Only a replica?" My heart sank somewhat at this news. "What happened to the real one?"

"If my memory serves, it rotted away. Drake sailed during Elizabeth the First's reign, which dates back to Shakespeare's time. In a way, I guess it fits today's mission."

"All roads lead back to Shakespeare," I joked. "It's impressive that they circumnavigated the globe on this. It's not that big. Nothing like a cruise ship."

"Cruise ships are so American." Her lips puckered, leaving little doubt about her low opinion of them, at least compared to English ships. I happened to agree. "Back to the literary connection, if my memory serves, there was a different replica of this same ship that was part of the British Empire Exhibition back in 1924, and it was used as a playground for children. It was Agatha Christie's suggestion. The one we're looking at now was constructed using traditional methods, and it has actually been used to sail real voyages. In fact, it once sailed to Japan to take part in the television production of *Shōgun*."

"Based on James Clavell's book?"

"Precisely. Yet another literary connection."

"Gosh." My eyelashes fluttered as all these marvelous facts sank in. "Every part of this city seems to have been a setting for a book or the home of a famous author. It's so cruel I'm only here for seventy-two hours."

"Completely barbaric, really. To truly absorb all that London has to offer, it's necessary to live here, at least temporarily."

I let out an anguished sigh, and Cleo gave me a funny smile that conveyed I was being overly dramatic without uttering a word. In my book, that counted as a real skill. She wasn't entirely wrong, though I felt it very important that I explain my reasoning so she could see I was mostly justified in my reaction.

"I admit I've dreamed of doing so, but moving to New York took so much out of me."

"Moving is always a challenge, though I've only moved flats myself, never cities."

"I moved thousands of miles, and my parents were not happy with my decision to be so far from home." I was surprised at how natural it felt to confide in her, even personal information about my family that I wouldn't normally share. "Believe it or not, my mother is convinced I'm going to die in some terrorist attack or something."

Cleo nodded, seeming to understand. "That could happen anywhere, though. Not that telling her that would make her feel better about it."

"Definitely not. And moving to a different country?" I cringed at the thought of the howl my mom would let out, something akin to a wild animal who'd lost a limb in a trap. "I think you'd hear her yelling at me all the way from here."

"I thought all Americans had pluck." Cleo gave an exaggerated pout.

"Pluck? I don't think that's in my DNA."

"You enjoy traveling, though," she pointed out.

"I do. I travel all over for my job."

"Ah, yes. The *job*." The way Cleo said it, it might as well have been a curse word. "And is that everything you dreamed it would be?"

"I like it well enough," I replied, stiffening ever so slightly at the judgment implied by her tone. "I don't have much choice where I go, at least not usually."

"You swoop in on unsuspecting stores around the world, going in for the kill?"

"I wouldn't call it a kill, and if I'm completely honest, the deal is usually already as good as done by the time I arrive. I go in to finalize the paperwork that brings the store officially under the Triple B umbrella. Usually, they're a lot more excited about it than you are, and I get to enjoy a trip that's all planned and paid for by the company." That was the best part of my job, but I suspected I shouldn't say this to Cleo, who was utterly convinced I hated my job, and stating this fact didn't exactly bolster my claim that I loved working for Triple B.

"But you miss being around stories and actually spending your days in a bookstore?"

I nodded. "More than I can explain."

"Do you ever see yourself working in a shop again? Or managing one, even?"

For the briefest moment, I could see myself standing in Braithwaite Books, carrying a stack of paperbacks as Sheila had done earlier, Cleo smiling from behind the counter as I went past. It was so startlingly clear in my mind, and my heart was so joyed by the vision my breath caught in my chest. I shook it off quickly, though. It was an insane thought, completely beyond the realm of possibility.

"A Triple B store, no. Unless I'm demoted, which might happen considering what a mess I'm making of this first solo sales meeting I was put in charge of."

Cleo pressed a hand to her chest. "You say that like it's my fault you're not doing your presentation right now."

"That's because it is," I shot back, though more jokingly than accusingly. "Can I tell you a secret?"

"Please do." Cleo clasped her hands together like an eager child, which I found ridiculously endearing despite the fact she really was contributing to my likely firing in the near future.

"I've always dreamed of running my own bookstore. A small shop. Nothing like Borders. I want a place like… well, to be frank, something like your place. That would be a dream come true."

"It certainly has been for me," Cleo said.

"I remember back in the day, when I was a kid, I would buy discount books and store them under my bed. I figured that way I'd already have some inventory." I laughed over this memory, and Cleo joined in. "I was such a dork."

"Do you still have those books?"

"At my parents' place. My apartment in New York is the size of a broom closet."

"At the price of a mansion in most parts of the world, I imagine," Cleo added. "Sadly, London isn't any better on that front."

"Maybe not, but look at all the history you get for your money," I said with a sigh. "It must be the next best thing to living inside a book."

Cleo nodded at my observation. "By the sound of it, books are in your blood."

"Yes, just not that can-do attitude you admire so much about Americans, I'm afraid." My stomach tightened as I thought of the carefully planned proposal I hadn't so much as started on yet. I'd had such high hopes for this trip, but so far, I was making a mess of things, even while simultaneously having the time of my life.

My stomach rumbled so loudly we both could hear it.

"Right. I can't help with the can-do attitude, but our next stop should take care of that situation." Cleo grinned, pointing to my noisy tummy.

I checked my phone for the time, surprised to find it was quite a bit later than I'd thought. How had it crept to two minutes after noon? As if to reinforce that nothing so far was going the way I'd envisioned, there were no new messages from Glory. In fact, the one I'd sent earlier remained unread. Despite the fun day I'd been having, this trip was quickly turning into a disaster on the work front. Now, I feared my personal life might be headed the same way.

CHAPTER FIFTEEN

WE LEFT the Golden Hinde in the rearview mirror, so to speak, as we headed to the next destination on Cleo's secret itinerary. Putting aside my unease about closing the deal, and my concern over not having heard back from Glory, I'd be lying if I said I wasn't curious what Cleo had up her sleeve next. So far, the day had held one glorious surprise after another.

I suspected my tour guide might have chosen another picturesque pub for us to eat in, but when we arrived, I discovered I was very much mistaken.

"Welcome to Borough Market." Cleo grinned as I took in the massive open-air space that seemed to house an entire city of food stands and shops beneath a crystal-clear glass roof. "It dates back to 1276, not in its present form, of course. It was probably more carts and wagons back then."

"That's over seven hundred years," I said, my brain

swimming as I tried to comprehend something being that old.

"In fact, many suspect it started much earlier. Perhaps in the eleventh century. It took its present form centuries later, and it's become an important food market due to its proximity to the wharves."

"So much history."

"That's just the icing on the cake. The best part of this market is wandering through and eating nibbles." She motioned for me to follow her. "Do you like cheese?"

"In my humble opinion, only crazy people don't." A waft of strong-smelling cheese washed over me, and my stomach rumbled like a wildebeest demanding to be sated. "No offense to vegans and the lactose intolerant, but seriously. I can barely contain myself right now."

"Then we'd best get started," Cleo said. We began at one end, reading the name of the cheese and taking a tiny morsel. While the pieces were small, the flavors burst in my mouth.

"I think I could live here!"

"In the market or London?" Cleo turned her inquisitive eyes on me.

"Not sure I'll ever be able to separate the two now."

"Of all the things I've shown you, this is the one that would make you move?"

I shrugged. "What can I say? That's how devoted I

am to cheese."

The next stall offered samples of sausages, and I was pretty sure I might have died and gone to heaven. A sizzling sound nabbed my attention as someone prepared food on a large grill. We stopped to watch for a minute, but there was so much to take in my eyes and ears had a hard time deciding where to focus.

"Welcome to Borough Market, love!" shouted a guy in what looked like a captain's hat. He was gesturing toward a mountain of ice, on top of which sat some of the largest oyster shells I'd ever seen.

"Shall we get some?" Cleo asked.

I pretended to swoon. "Oysters are like cheese. I never say no."

We ordered one each, which was plenty since they were larger than the size of my hand. I watched the man struggling some as he grasped the beast in his blue-gloved hand and inserted the metal instrument to pop the shell.

Moving to a table, we sat down.

"Do we use a knife and fork?" I asked, not feeling overly confident how to tackle this sea monster.

"You can if you'd like," Cleo said with a shrug that to my mind came across as a challenge. "I like to tip the shell and get it in one go." She held the shell—which honestly looked more like a cereal bowl—and tipped it into her mouth. She had to focus to get it all in, nearly losing the entire thing, but she did, indeed, succeed in slurping it in at the last second.

"Impressive."

Wiping her mouth with the back of her hand, she said, "Go on. You can do it."

An audience was gathering, all eyes on me. I'd never been a fan of being the center of attention, so I kept my eyes on Cleo, like a ship captain looking for the lighthouse on a stormy night, feeling a sense of comfort washing over me. It was strange how calming I found her presence.

"Here goes nothing." I tried getting it into my mouth, having to reposition the shell several times. The oyster sloshed around in its juices. I leaned down, fearful all was lost, but in the end, I beat it.

Cleo let out an excited yip. Taking a paper napkin, she wiped the juices off my chin. Her fingers brushed the edge of my mouth, and a tingling moved through me. Our eyes locked, and I let out the most contented sigh that'd ever escaped my mouth. I should have been mortified, but I wasn't.

"Have you had your fill?" Cleo asked quietly. "Or are you still hungry?"

"I'm not sure I'll ever be done here." The smells of so many delicious foods filled my senses, but deep down, I wondered if it was only the food I was talking about. Nothing could come of it, of course, but part of me wished I could extend this day with Cleo and make it last forever.

"That's what I like to hear," Cleo said, oblivious to any of my deeper and less appropriate thoughts. "Let's go to one of the oldest vendors and share one of their classic dishes. Eggs, black pudding, bacon, sausages, and bubble and squeak."

"I know eggs, bacon, and sausages, but what the heck is black pudding? And did you say bubble and squeak? That sounds like something you'd feed a Beatrix Potter character."

"Bubble and squeak is fried potatoes and cabbage, so maybe not as enchanting as you think but still very good. It's probably best if I don't tell you what black pudding is until after you try it."

"That sounds ominous."

She waggled her brows at me, and I laughed even as emotions deep inside me stirred. There was definitely something intriguing about this woman. If only we'd met under different circumstances.

While Cleo ordered, I tackled the crowds, which were elbow to elbow in the most congested parts of the market, to find a place for us to sit. I waved triumphantly to two chairs at a table with a green and white checkered covering. Cleo hurried over and set the plate down between us.

"Nicely done," she said, letting out a grateful sigh as she sat down. "I recommend adding brown sauce to the bubble and squeak."

"Brown sauce?"

"Think of it like ketchup, but it has a spicier tang." Cleo picked up a plastic bottle and squirted out a deep brown liquid almost like a barbecue sauce. Then she handed me a fork. I took a hesitant bite.

"It reminds me of A1 steak sauce." My next bite wasn't so timid, bringing a smile to Cleo's lips. "Where's the bacon?"

She pointed to a slab of meat that looked more like ham.

"That's different, but so far, I haven't disliked anything." I nibbled on a bite. "Not bad."

"Are you ready for the true challenge?"

My eyes became flying-saucer size, or at least I think they did due to the amount of oxygen burning my retinas. "What sort of challenge did you have in mind?"

"Try a bit of the black pudding." She pointed to a circular slab of... something.

I wrinkled my nose. "It doesn't look like the pudding we have back home."

"No chocolate in it, that's for sure."

"It really is black." I forked off a bite from the disc, slowly raising it to my mouth. "This isn't a trick, is it? Like this is just for show? No one's supposed to eat it?"

"It's not parsley!" Her features softened, and I was struck by the kindness in her eyes. "It's something you should try at least once if you want the true English food experience. I'd never lead you astray."

Our eyes locked, and her sentiment about never leading me astray rolled around in my head. I trusted her completely, and I suspected it might run deeper than just food. It defied explanation.

If my sampling of bubble and squeak was hesitant, my black pudding morsel couldn't really be counted as a valid effort, but the repulsiveness of the color and consistency was at odds with my desire to live up to Cleo's perception of a can-do American.

I slowly chewed a minuscule crumb, expecting something truly terrible. Instead, I discovered it had an earthy flavor. Not something I could pin down, exactly, but not bad. I tried another bite, a little larger this time, chewing more slowly still.

"You like it?"

"I'm on the fence," I said. "It's different. Not something I'd crave, but… edible."

Even though my words were tepid, Cleo's smile spread ear to ear. "That's the spirit. I knew there was an adventurous side in you. I just knew it!"

"Are you going to tell me what's in it?"

"Not right now. Let's finish this and head to the last stop. In the market, that is," she quickly added. "Our tour's nowhere near done. We still have miles to go until we sleep."

I felt a thrill at the prospect of whatever was ahead, marveling at how perfectly Cleo had planned the day. She was a remarkable woman, the type I'd waited my whole life to meet. I'd nearly lost faith she existed, yet here she was. Had I ever spent a nicer day or in better company?

"I wish the day could go on forever," I sighed.

It took several seconds for me to remember my dinner plans that night with Glory were the reason the day would have to end, and when I did, I had to swallow a piece of sausage to staunch the guilt.

"Since you were such a good sport about the black pudding," Cleo said, "I think a treat is in order."

She might not think I was so deserving if she'd been aware of the internal battle suddenly raging within. How could I so thoroughly enjoy this time with her when I was supposed to be with someone else? I didn't deserve a treat at all. I deserved to be punished for my fickleness, and for how quickly I'd abandoned my work ethic and loyalty in the face of pleasurable company and a pretty smile. I told myself I would begin fasting immediately. No more temptation for me. I would be monk-like in my repentance and self-denial.

Except, the treat turned out to be a chocolate-filled donut, the outside sprinkled with sugar. This wasn't the type of thing I could say no to, no matter how guilty I felt. I would've made a terrible monk.

I took one bite, and tears of joy flooded my eyes. "I think I'm in love... with this donut."

If she picked up on my moment of hesitation, Cleo didn't show any sign of it. I might not be good at denying myself, but it turned out I was an expert at denial.

CHAPTER SIXTEEN

"THIS IS SOUTHWARK CATHEDRAL." Cleo made a ta-da motion with her hands, and I smiled, though my heart wasn't in it. Ever since we'd left Borough Market, which was still in sight, the extent to which I'd deviated from my original mission had been weighing on me. "It's the oldest Gothic church in London. Given its proximity to The Globe—"

"Did Shakespeare come here?" I asked, blushing slightly as I realized I'd interrupted.

Cleo studied my face briefly, scanning it as if to discover the source of my sudden change in mood, but she didn't press the issue. "Come inside and find out."

I hesitated, earning me another questioning look.

"I'm not planning to hurt you, Marley."

Perhaps not, I thought as I tailed her into the church, but when this day reached its end, I feared it would hurt one or both of us very much. Neither of us intended it to, but there it was.

This woman, for so many unknown reasons, lit up my insides in a way I'd never experienced before. I had no idea why. Okay, I did know at least one of the reasons. This amazing tour she'd spontaneously taken me on was like the fulfillment of a childhood dream that never dimmed in my adult years.

I was not spontaneous by nature. The spreadsheets Cleo so maligned were what I lived for, logical and planned. The last time I had acted spontaneously was when I didn't have any food in my apartment and ordered Domino's pizza. Much to my shame because New York has some of the best places in the world to choose from, but I didn't want to leave my apartment, and Domino's was familiar and comforting. I couldn't even do spontaneity right. But with Cleo, it felt so different, an exhilarating rush that breathed life into everything around me.

"These stained glass windows are dedicated to the bard, who is the most well-known parishioner of Southwark." Cleo tilted her head to take them in like she'd never seen them before. I admired this quality about her. No way would she settle for shitty pizza.

"It's probably safe to say Shakespeare is the most well-known in just about any category."

"Oh, Dickens is a close second, but to explore places he visited, we'd have to meet up again."

"Maybe that could be arranged." I avoided her eyes,

taking in the stained glass, unable to believe I'd said that out loud. I wasn't even sure why I had. The rest of my time in London was promised to Glory.

"Wouldn't it be lovely if we could keep exploring together?" she asked, my heart clenching at the suggestion. "I want to show you why London is special. Why I love my bookshop that celebrates this amazing city and the authors who transport us into their stories, giving us a piece of them. I love your curiosity. It's infectious. Believe it or not, I'm only showing you a small slice since we're on foot. Think of how much more there is to see!"

"I—" I wanted so badly to say yes, to ditch my plans and obligations and ride off into the great unknown with this woman I barely knew. It seemed every two steps brought another amazing find to light. But ditching plans wasn't in Marley Royce's DNA, or it hadn't been until Cleo Braithwaite got me to play hooky. I sighed, my heart heavy. "I'm sorry, Cleo. I'm having a wonderful time, but it's after lunch, and we haven't talked about business for even a minute. I can't keep neglecting my duties like this."

Cleo's lips pressed into a thin line, making me fear I'd offended her, but then she nodded. "What do you suggest?"

"We're still near the Globe Theatre, right?" A current of excitement made my fingers prickle, both because of our proximity to such a famous location and also because it gave me the perfect idea for how to get this day back on track, professionally speaking, anyway. "There's a Triple B bookstore around the corner. It was acquired in July. I was supposed to travel here for the closing, but I had to cancel at the last minute. Even so, I'm familiar with the proposal, and I'm certain it would be the perfect way to demonstrate to you why you should sign with us, without all those spreadsheets and slides you hate so much."

Hesitation flickered in Cleo's eyes. For a few seconds, I thought she might turn me down, but finally, she relented. "I suppose it's inevitable. Lead the way."

I grinned in triumph. "You won't regret it. Given the location is so close to Shakespeare's stomping grounds, this shop will be a shrine, a temple to classical literature."

"You really think so?" she sounded completely baffled by my statement.

"Absolutely." I frowned, my eyes flicking down one side of the street and then the other. "Just one thing. Can you lead us there? I have no idea where I'm going. It's—"

"Oh, I know it." Without another word, she led the way.

CHAPTER SEVENTEEN

"Here it is." Cleo's tone was flat, her face devoid of expression, as we arrived at the new acquisition. It was the least animated I'd seen her all day, which struck me as strange given that we were about to enter a bookshop. Was she the jealous type, a shopkeeper who couldn't stand to be around her competition?

I clasped my hands together as I took in the shop's stone front with the three interlocking Bs on the sign above the door. "I'm as excited to see it in person as I am to show it to you."

"You've never seen it?" she asked.

I shook my head. "Not even in photos. Unfortunately, once the deal is done, I move onto the next thing. I never get to see the final results, although I read the proposals so I know what's been planned."

"And you feel this shop is a good representation of

Triple B's work?" Something in her expression made me hesitate, suddenly unsure.

"I… I think so." I cleared my throat, my confidence returning. Other than Braithwaite Books, this location had been the most sought-after prize in London. "If anything will show you what Triple B can do for your shop, this will be it. I don't know why I didn't think of this earlier. You ready to be dazzled?"

Cleo grasped the door and pulled it open, motioning for me to go first. "In that case, let's take a look-see."

It took a few moments for my surroundings to hit me. When they did, I blinked rapidly, as if waiting for my eyes to adjust after stepping into a dark room. If only bad lighting had been the problem.

Though the exterior had all the charm of old London, the illusion evaporated at the door. Inside, the walls were stark white, industrial carpeting covering the floor, with bins of books laid out in rows like some sort of bargain basement.

My jaw dropped, and I attempted to laugh off my shock. "Clearly, the renovations haven't started yet."

Cleo wasn't laughing. Instead, her eyes looked sad. "Take a deep breath, Marley. What do you smell?"

I breathed in as she'd requested, and it hit me.

Fresh paint.

"I don't understand," I stammered, unable to make sense of what my eyes and nose were telling me. The walls had recently been painted. Upon closer inspection, the carpet, too, was new. "We must have the wrong location."

"It's the right place." Cleo wrapped her hand around my bent elbow, gently nudging me toward the door. "Let's talk about this somewhere else."

Tears stung my eyes as I followed her out. As soon as the fresh air hit my nostrils, I took a deep, cleansing breath to rid myself of the terrible chemical smell. "What is going on in there? It's not at all the way it's supposed to be. I remember the plans so clearly."

Taking a step closer, Cleo cradled my face with a hand on each cheek. She looked deeply into my eyes for an eternity, and her expression could only be described as relief. "You really didn't know about Triple B."

I shook my head as much as I could while her hands continued to hold it in place. All the while my stomach plummeted as I wondered exactly how ignorant I had been. The way she looked at me made all the hair on my body stand up. Not out of fear, or even excitement, but something more.

Or else I was simply overwhelmed by the turn of events after everything.

Yes, that was it. It had to be, right? After what I'd seen, I knew my chances of signing Braithwaite Books was dead. But I had to keep to the rest of my plan. I had to meet Glory. Only, suddenly, I didn't think I could. Perhaps I felt unworthy.

"What thoughts are going through your head? Your

eyes have gone a bit cloudy." Cleo's expression turned to worry.

"Everything is starting to hit me. I had so much riding on this trip. I—" I took a ragged breath, fighting back panic. "I think I need a drink."

CHAPTER EIGHTEEN

WITHOUT ANOTHER WORD, Cleo placed her hand on my elbow and steered us away from the abomination of a bookshop, directly to the nearest pub, a place called The Mudlark. She plopped me at a table inside and headed to the bar. Within minutes, she returned with two half-pints. They'd been a novelty earlier in the day, but given my current mood, I wished they were American-sized.

"What does mudlark mean?" I asked, not yet ready to discuss the garbled thoughts in my head.

The ghost of a smile on her lips told me she knew I was stalling but wasn't going to press. How was it I'd finally met such a wonderful, understanding woman? Of course, that it had happened the same day I had a date with someone else and also found out my job was a complete sham was par for the course where my luck was concerned.

"It's the term for people who scour river mud for treasures," she answered, her voice soft.

"Do people still do that?"

"I think so." It was unlike Cleo not to possess an encyclopedia's worth of knowledge behind any random piece of trivia that came up, so I knew the fact she hadn't delved into a full history meant something was off. Or maybe she was being kind and realized my brain wasn't up to the task of listening.

Once I'd finished about half my miniature beer, she prodded me with, "Well? Are you ready to talk?"

At this point, I realized her refusing to go off on a tangent before was because she intended to put me on the hot seat and didn't want to be distracted from her goal.

I let out a shaky sigh. It was the last thing I wanted to discuss, but part of me needed to. "They've been lying to me all along."

She nodded, and I was relieved not to see any judgement in her eyes, though I still blamed myself. "It wasn't only you they lied to."

This hardly made me feel better. "I'm the one who does the dirty work, though. I'm the one who has repeated their lies like they were truths."

"You have a trustworthiness to you, an earnestness that makes you ideal for the job. Triple B used that to its advantage."

No wonder she'd hated me so when I'd first

arrived, or what I represented, anyway. She must have thought I was in on their deception this whole time. That made me feel oh so dirty.

"You have to believe me. I had no idea. Usually, my job is so simple. The sale is already in the bag. My role has been to reassure owners that the company will keep the spirit of their shops while also making them better, because that's what I believed was going to happen."

"You had no way of knowing." Considering I'd been sent to hoodwink her, she was being awfully nice to me, much more so than I deserved. It made me feel even worse.

"How many times have I said the only thing we'll change is the profit? They'll still be in charge, but they'll have more resources? Triple B only wants to help them succeed?" I tensed my jaw, wishing I could scream. "It's all a crock of shit. None of it's true, is it?"

"From what I've seen, no."

Tears threatened to fall, and it took all I had to keep them in check. If only I hadn't been so eager to be sent on this trip, I wouldn't have had to face the truth. Now that I knew, I was screwed.

I narrowed my eyes, regarding Cleo with suspicion. "Why did you agree to this meeting?"

She knitted her brow. "What do you mean?"

"You have a beautiful shop, chockfull of character. If you want it to remain that way, you can't sign with

Triple B, and you had to have known that from the start. Why did you agree to meet with Triple B? And what's more, why did you request me specifically?" A coldness settled into the pit of my stomach. The future, so bright only that morning, was dim. "Now that I know what they're up to, I can't keep playing along. I can never go on working for a company like this. I've lost my career."

"I'm sorry." She drank her beer, looking out the window. "Perhaps I should've gone about this a different way. This puts you in a bad spot, and I'll admit I didn't think it through."

I remained silent, not sure what to say. Neither one of us was in a great spot. I would soon be out of a job, but I'd seen the financial data for her shop, and the numbers didn't lie. We were both in deep doo-doo.

To my surprise, when Cleo turned her head from the window, she wore an odd, excited smile. "The truth is I accepted this meeting because I've been looking for someone like you for so long."

"Me?" I leaned a bit over the table, enthralled by those pink lips of hers and overcome with a sudden desire to find out how soft they were. Was it possible she felt the same?

"Can I ask if you feel the connection as well?" Her voice was barely a whisper as she ran her finger along the brim of her glass.

My heart pounded like a jackhammer. I couldn't

believe I'd heard her correctly, and all of a sudden, I was painfully shy. I swallowed, trying to avoid her eyes and those long lashes. Words wouldn't form in my brain, so I simply nodded, terrified and exhilarated at what would happen next.

CHAPTER NINETEEN

"I NEED YOU." Cleo's breathy voice sent shivers down my spine. I don't know what I expected to happen next. Maybe I pictured her leaning across the table to kiss me or making a heartfelt declaration of devotion. Instead, Cleo sat back in her chair, clasping her hands together, and grinned. "I love beginnings. Don't you?"

"Er... yes?"

"It's the best reason to open a book. Not the only reason, but there's that anticipation, right from the very first line." She closed her eyes. *Last night I dreamt I went to Manderley again.* I started rereading that one the other day. Pure genius."

"I love Daphne Du Maurier," I offered, sounding as dazed as I felt.

"*Rebecca* is her finest in my opinion."

I nodded, biting my lip. We were back to talking

about books, and I had no idea where this conversation was going. Don't get me wrong, I love books, but I was too confused at that moment to remember a single story I'd ever read, much less start quoting from one.

"Um, what's beginning?" I asked, feeling like an idiot. Was there a declaration of love on the horizon? With the sudden shift in mood, the suspicion was growing in my breast that we were on very different pages where romance was concerned.

"Our collaboration, of course."

Collaboration. What an un-sexy word. Here I'd thought we were connecting on an intimate level, but Cleo seemed to have business on the brain and nothing more. *Which is a good thing,* I reminded myself as my dinner with Glory came rushing back to me. How did I keep forgetting that simple fact?

"Can you run all of this by me again?" My heart raced, and my hands went clammy with guilt. "Slowly, please."

Instead of complying, Cleo took several swallows of beer, until I thought I might scream. The glass only held eight ounces. How long could it take to finish? Just when I thought I might pass out, she set her empty drink on the table and looked me square in the eye.

"I need your help righting my shop. I'm not looking for company secrets." She quickly added, "Just for you to point me on the right path."

"Like a consultant?"

"Exactly. It's no secret managing the shop is not in my blood. I love the people aspect, not the numbers. Show me a spreadsheet, and my eyes glaze over. I'd rather pluck out all of my eyelashes."

"That would be a travesty. You have beautiful eyelashes." Oh God. I had not meant to say that in my outside voice. As my temperature skyrocketed, I wished there was a way to suck those words back into my head.

"I do?" Cleo batted her lashes, but I didn't think she was doing it intentionally. That didn't stop it from having an effect on me.

Which it absolutely should not have had. I couldn't allow it to continue. Cleo had made it more than clear the only thing on her mind was a business arrangement. I'd as good as lost my job already, but there was so much more at stake if I screwed things up with Glory, too.

"Would you excuse me for a minute?" I fled to the bathroom with my bag, needing a moment. When the door was safely closed, I pulled out my phone, desperate for something to ground me, but Glory still had not responded to my earlier text, and the signal in the bathroom was too weak to send her another in hopes of catching her attention.

"Get it together," I whispered to my reflection in the bathroom mirror. I breathed in deeply, imagining as I blew out the air that all my inappropriate thoughts about Cleo Braithwaite were leaving with it. When my blood pressure had stabilized and my libido was under control, I returned to the table.

"What exactly do you have in mind?" I made a point of avoiding those hypnotic eyes, not wanting to fall in again.

"I think together we'd make a great pair. I don't want to be the Braithwaite that loses the shop. I may not care about the business side of things, but I care deeply about the business, nonetheless. If I lose that…" Her voice quavered, and she looked down at the table. I reached out on sheer impulse, smothering her hand with mine. "I don't know how to explain this, and what I'm about to say is probably complete bollocks, but I can't shake this feeling that you're the missing puzzle piece."

"I—?"

My voice gave out on me. This didn't feel like business, and I wasn't sure what to do about that. I pulled my hand away from hers.

"Don't say no," she urged, almost as if she could read the doubt in my mind. "Not right now. Think it over."

CHAPTER TWENTY

CLEO PICKED up her beer glass, frowned as she examined its empty state, and then emphatically set it down. "Ready to shove off? There's so much of the city to see, and I still have you for a few more hours. I hope I haven't scared you off."

"Absolutely not," I assured her, which was mostly true. Even with all the emotions swirling around inside, I couldn't say no to more sightseeing. I loved this city, and Cleo was the best tour guide a girl could want. I had to remind myself that was all she was, a business associate with an enviable knowledge of London.

I took a fortifying breath.

We stepped out of the pub, the sunlight causing me to place a hand over my eyes as I asked, "Did Charles Dickens lie?"

"What do you mean?" Her laugh made it sound

like that was the most ridiculous, but also the most brilliant, question she'd ever heard.

"His books are full of fog, rain, and misery. But, it's so bloody bright here."

"You said *bloody*. I love it!" She clapped her hands together and spun around.

"It's odd that's the word that gets you so excited." Despite my confusion, I laughed, too, happy to feel a return to the easy camaraderie we'd enjoyed earlier in the day before my brain had gone all haywire.

After a short walk, we started to cross a bridge, heading back to the northern side of the Thames.

"What do you think of this bridge?" Cleo stopped long enough to tap her foot three times.

I peered beyond the side of the cement bridge and then leaned over to get a better glimpse of the structure spanning the river. "Well, if I'm being honest, it's not the most impressive thing I've seen today."

"I agree."

"Which bridge is it, anyway?"

"London Bridge."

My jaw dropped. "This can't possibly be one of the most famous bridges in the entire world."

"I assure you it is, although it's not the original," she said. "If you want to see that one, you have to travel to Arizona."

"Arizona? Like the one in America?"

"That's the one. Back in the sixties, it was determined the bridge had to be replaced because it was sinking into the river. Fixing it would be too costly. A city councilor proposed selling the bridge. An American millionaire had recently purchased a lot of land around Lake Havasu and wanted something special to draw people to visit. We were selling one of the largest antiques…" She shrugged.

"You've got to be kidding me."

"Not at all. They shipped it there, stone by stone and put it back together." Cleo's eyes twinkled in that conspiratorial way she had that I'd come to find so charming. "There's a rumor that the millionaire thought he was buying Tower Bridge, but he vehemently denied it."

"That's the really fancy one, right?" I stroked my chin as Cleo nodded. "I think I would lie, too, if I messed that up."

"Would you, now?"

"Usually, I can admit a mistake," I said. "But buying the wrong bridge? That would be a tough one to cop to. Would you be willing to admit to the entire world that you'd fucked up that badly?"

"No! I'd do my best tap dancing to prove to the world I wasn't the biggest idiot on the planet." She actually did a little tap dance right on the spot, making me laugh, and I had to wonder if she was putting on more of a show because she suspected her proclamation earlier hadn't been the type I wanted to hear.

CHAPTER TWENTY-ONE

WE WERE WALKING along a busy sidewalk, and Cleo kept her brisk pace, dodging and darting through the crowd. Her need to keep moving made me think if she stopped, everything would come falling down around her.

Falling down, falling down...

Great. Now I had the nursery rhyme "London Bridge is Falling Down" swirling around in my head. Just what the day was missing, an annoying song to get tangled up with all the whirling thoughts in my head.

We weren't far past the bridge when my eye caught a glimpse of a massive column to my left, with something golden glinting on top like a flame. I called out Cleo's name, but she didn't hear over the rumbling of busses and black cabs, so eventually I resorted to tugging on her shirt.

"What's that?" I asked, letting the fabric of her peasant blouse drop from my fingers, but not before making a mental note of how soft it was and oh so pleasant to touch.

"Where?" She looked perplexed, but not upset as I'd feared she might be by my taking liberties, however small, with her clothing. Then again, she may not have perceived it that way. Between the two of us, I was the only one who seemed to be unable to keep my mind from straying beyond the boundaries of work.

"That, there." I pointed to the unknown structure, suddenly grateful to have a distraction.

"Oh, that." A shadow passed over Cleo's features, and she didn't elaborate or even tell me the name of the thing. How very odd.

"Are you okay?" I asked before I could question whether that was an appropriate thing to do.

"Fine," she said, not very convincingly. "I forgot all about *that*."

"You still haven't said what it is," I pointed out.

"It's the Monument to the Great Fire of London." Cleo's tone was flat, and there was a flicker of uneasiness in her usually merry eyes.

I wasn't sure what was odder, that Cleo was so skittish around this monument or that she wasn't trying to hide it. If I was a betting woman, I would put my life savings on there being more to this story. Although, considering how little money I had saved and my looming unemployment status, that wasn't such a huge gamble. Still, I was curious.

"Here it is." Cleo made an exaggerated ta-da gesture at the monument, but there was something off about her delivery. "Remember when we were at the Anchor pub?"

"That was the first one across the river?" It seemed like days ago, but it'd only been a couple of hours.

She nodded, pointing in that general direction. "Samuel Pepys, the diarist, watched the fire from there, and this column commemorates the fire."

My eyes followed the column from the base toward the sky, reinforcing why this structure caught my attention because it seemed to keep going up. Now that we were closer, I could see the top was a golden urn, which did, indeed, appear to have flames coming out of it.

"It's built on the site where the first church was destroyed by the fire." Cleo's tone was somber, reverent even. She looked like she was seeing ghosts.

"Can we go to the top?"

"Er, yes, but I don't recommend it."

"Why?" I checked out the blue sky. "I bet the view would be fantastic."

"I'm sure it is, but there are over three hundred steps. That's a lot of climbing, especially if you still want to try to do St. Paul's." For someone who radiated energy, I found it odd she didn't want to tackle this challenge, but not being overly fond of stairs myself, I didn't press.

"Are you afraid of heights?" Okay, I couldn't help but press a little.

"Not exactly. I just prefer—this one spooks me a little, truth be known."

"Why?" Her answer was so starkly honest it caught me by surprise.

"The truth?" Cleo shuddered. "I'm terrified of fire."

"Surely, they weren't stupid enough to tempt fate with an eternal flame up there." I glanced back up at the gold on top.

"No, they didn't. I think it would be in poor taste if they did."

"Good point." I was tempted to laugh the whole thing off, but Cleo still looked spooked. Before I could remind myself that such behavior wasn't strictly professional, I rested a hand on her shoulder. "I'm sorry I made us stop. You should've told me no."

"It's not your fault. I can't explain it, but I've never been able to walk past this monument without an eerie feeling." She took a step back, and I don't think it was intentional. Her fear was in charge. "I can't bring myself to climb to the top. Not even when all my class-mates did it years ago."

"Some things do scare you, then?"

"Of course. And not only fire."

"Losing your business?" I guessed.

"That most of all." She swallowed, her expression

grim. "There was one other time in our history when Braithwaite's teetered on the brink of ruin. Because of a fire, interestingly enough."

"The Great Fire of London?"

"The old girl's not that ancient," she said, a ghost of a smile on her lips. "The London fire was in 1666, when the founder of Braithwaite's was still in nappies. Although I'm willing to concede we might as well be that old, for as outdated as we've become."

"You really are nervous about the future." It hit me for the first time exactly how much she had to lose. Sure, I was soon to be out of a job now that I knew the truth about my employer the bookstore cannibalizer, for lack of a better word, but Cleo was on the verge of losing her family's legacy.

"You'll find I'm a bundle of nerves about all sorts of things." That darkness in her sparkling eyes briefly flared, but her laughter knocked it out. "However, I'm British, so I shove everything deep down."

"Everything?"

Her eyes locked on mine so intensely my toes tingled. "Almost everything."

CHAPTER TWENTY-TWO

"SHALL WE MOVE ON?" Cleo waved for us to retrace our steps back to the road we'd been on before this unfortunate detour.

"As long as we can talk on the way to wherever we're heading," I said, trying to keep my tone casual. I must not have done a good job of it because Cleo inclined her head to one side, studying me much more closely than was comfortable.

"We've been talking the entire day," she said.

"Something's changed since your proposal." We fell into step, side by side.

"I hope I didn't scare you. I should have waited a bit longer, but I tend to blurt things out when it's not the right time. You were still in shock after seeing the Triple B store. I should have let that wash over you."

"Does that mean you don't want me to help with

your shop?" A sharp pang of disappointment caught me by surprise.

"Don't think that for a second. It doesn't mean that at all. I knew the moment I laid eyes on you that you're the one I've been waiting for."

"For your business." I said this more for my own benefit, a reminder of where things stood. Honestly, since that was all she had in mind, I wished she'd stop using language that made my heart pirouette around on tippy-toe.

"Yeah." She didn't sound entirely sure, and her shrug only reinforced the idea she was bluffing or truly didn't understand her own motivations. "Naturally, that's what I was talking about."

"Why me?"

"For one thing, you have a lot more experience in this industry."

"You're conveniently forgetting I'm working for an evil corporation that destroys whatever it touches. You admitted as much." A man in a suit jostled my side, making me bump into Cleo. The heat singed my skin, only ramping up my confusion. "I still don't understand what you want me to do, exactly."

"I need fresh ideas and a plan for implementing them." If Cleo had even noticed how our bodies had touched, she didn't let on. "I need someone who lights up whenever I mention anything about books."

"I don't light up." I turned my attention to a red double-decker bus rumbling by, still rattled by how very aware of Cleo's presence I was in every inch of my body.

"You absolutely do!" Cleo's carefree enthusiasm had returned, and she nudged me with her shoulder.

"Okay, for the sake of argument, let's say I do. How does that qualify me for this job any more than you? You love books, too, and you're still—" I stopped, my body going cold as I realized there was no nice way to put it.

"Failing miserably?" Cleo suggested, filling in the unfortunate blank I'd created. It relieved me that she didn't sound upset by my heartless stupidity.

"I wouldn't say it like that," I argued, but except for semantics, that was an outright lie. Without some drastic changes, Braithwaite's was dying, if not already dead. How was little old me supposed to breathe life back into it?

"Would you say this? Without help, I'll have to shut the doors within a year."

"Uh… yeah," I agreed.

More like six months.

Cleo stopped on the sidewalk, moving to the side, tugging me with her to avoid us being crushed by other pedestrians. "That's a step in the right direction."

"What is?"

"You didn't soften the blow. I don't want you to. I don't need someone to lie to me. I need someone to roll up their sleeves and help me."

"I'm only the paperwork gal."

"Are you telling me that in your fancy PowerPoint presentation, there aren't slides saying what Triple B would do to save the shop?"

"There are, but you're missing the point." Our bodies were nearly touching, her scent tickling my nose and distracting my already addled brain. "When I quit Triple B, I won't have those resources to pour into the shop. I'll only have my knowledge."

"I have to believe that will be enough."

"I…" There was so much hope in her eyes I wanted to cry. I wished I could pull her close to me and tell her I could save the day. I wasn't sure it was true, though. "I think another pub stop is in order."

CHAPTER TWENTY-THREE

I WASN'T THIRSTY, and after the two half-pints I'd enjoyed earlier in the day, I wasn't desperate for alcohol or anything. What I needed was a chance to focus my head on business, away from all thoughts of rescuing this beautiful damsel in distress.

"There's a pub up ahead. You're never far from a proper drink." Her expression dimmed. "Although, it's half past two. We won't be able to dawdle long."

"I thought that was the purpose of this day." I slowed my step, one arm behind my back.

Cleo quirked an eyebrow. "Is that your version of dawdling or figure skating?"

"It can't be figure skating," I told her with a laugh, "because I'm not nearly wobbly enough. Growing up in Minnesota, you'd think I would've mastered skating, but you would be wrong."

"It must be dawdling, then." She held a slender

finger in the air. "I should've expected as much."

"What reason do I have to dawdle?" Even as I asked, I could think of one good reason. The afternoon was ticking away, and soon it would be time to say goodbye. Anything I could do to make the day stretch out a little longer was worth a shot no matter how foolish I looked.

Cleo stopped in front of the door to a pub. A sign on the front said The Sugarloaf. I eyed the building, which was brick up top, but the pub portion was painted black. As Cleo rested her hand on the knob, she gave me a thoughtful look but didn't answer my question. Instead, she opened the door and held it for me.

"This doesn't seem all that sugary," I told her when we were inside. "Although, all the colorful flowers on the exterior take the bite out of the blackness."

"This is one of the best tips I can offer for when you need to find a pub in a hurry," Cleo said. "Look for a place with flowers, particularly hanging baskets. Those are a good indication it's a pub."

"Why's that?" I asked. "I would've thought flowers would indicate a florist."

"Apparently, it's all part of an effort on the part of pubs to become more Instagrammable. There's a place in Kensington that spends thirty thousand pounds a year on flowers, so I hear. Many places swap out the baskets with the season or for popular occasions, like a royal wedding or a holiday."

"They want 'grammers to snap away. I hadn't thought of that." We walked to the bar, my mind blurring with possibilities.

"What's going on in that brain?" Cleo asked before turning to the bartender. "Two halves of Harp."

"What if we tried it?" I replied.

"Tried what?"

"Upping the social media appeal of Braithwaite's. Your store is adorable inside, but what if we played that up even more?"

"With baskets of flowers?"

"Not flowers. I'm thinking, though. A friend of mine was here a handful of years ago and was tickled to discover a Paddington Bear trail."

"Yes, I recall that. With the shop being so close to Paddington Station, it was hard to avoid."

"Avoiding it is the exact opposite of what you should've done," I scolded. "Many businesses got involved, sponsoring stops on the trail. One was located in Hamleys—"

"Did you know their original store was destroyed by a fire in the early twentieth century?" After the bartender set down the drinks, Cleo swiped the glasses into her hands, motioning with her elbow for us to head to a table by a window.

I couldn't help chuckling. "You really do hate fire, don't you?"

"I have to check the hob three times before I can leave my flat."

"Hob? Is that what we call a stove?"

She nodded, sipping her drink. "Back to those Paddington Bears. If I remember correctly, it was to promote the movie, and they auctioned off the bears for charity. How can Braithwaite do something like that? We don't make movies, nor do we have a famous mascot."

"Why wasn't there a Paddington Bear in your shop?"

"Mum said no." She shook her head slowly, and I could see the importance of what I was saying beginning to sink in. "A missed opportunity."

"But there will be others." I gave her an encouraging smile. "We need to network more with other shops in the city to make the most of it the next time something like this rolls around."

"Did you say *we*?" She cupped an ear teasingly. "Does that mean you're accepting my offer?"

"I was using the universal we."

Cleo laughed. "No, you weren't. Admit it. You're tempted..."

Between the sexy way she let her sentence trail off and that alluring eyebrow arch, I was tempted, indeed. Cleo Braithwaite had the most luscious lips I'd ever encountered, and those penetrating eyes delightfully tortured my insides. The compulsion to lean in for a kiss was growing stronger by the second, an issue that was rapidly reaching its boiling point.

CHAPTER TWENTY-FOUR

CLEO MOVED CLOSER from across the table, her blouse shifting to offer an enticing view of her cleavage. My throat went dry, and I did my best not to look.

"I need to use the loo," she said, instantly catapulting me out of the land of fantasies and back to the present moment.

"Right, okay," I stammered like a fool.

The minute she was gone, I drained my beer in two gulps. This had been my third serving, but when I did the math, I'd only had one and a half beers. With lunch, I barely had a buzz. Two businessmen tumbled in the front door, shouting something about Arsenal, which I was pretty sure was a soccer team. It helped to dispel the last bit of magic, otherwise known as wishful thinking, surrounding the moment with Cleo right before she'd dashed away.

What the hell was wrong with me? I'd known Cleo

less than a day, and it was like I'd fallen under a spell. No one had ever had this effect on me.

Except Glory, I reminded myself.

Almost the exact second I thought her name, my phone buzzed with an incoming text. I scrambled to retrieve the device, my heart fluttering as I spied the tiny avatar I so loved.

Love, I repeated to myself, just in case I hadn't gotten it the first time. Cleo was a wonderful woman, and under any other circumstances... Well, it didn't matter because there weren't other circumstances. Glory texting was the perfect reminder.

I opened the text, biting my lip as I read, a sinking feeling weighing down on my chest.

I'm not sure if I can make it after all.

What?

No!

My hand was shaking as I texted her back. *What's wrong? Why not?*

But there was no response.

"You okay?"

I jumped at Cleo's voice. I'd been so focused on my phone I hadn't noticed her return. "It's nothing. Just catching up on some email from the office."

"No wonder you look so sour," Cleo commented. I thought she might press the issue for a moment, but she didn't. Instead, she said, "We should get going, or we'll miss the surprise."

"This day has been full of them," I offered.

From the ashes of Glory's disappointing text, hope was rising that before the end of the day, Cleo and I could reignite that intimate moment we'd experienced before. But if the chance arose, was that really what I wanted?

CHAPTER TWENTY-FIVE

WE WERE on a street parallel to the river, and given the increase of people rushing hither and thither, I guessed we were heading toward a more crowded part of the city, but the final destination remained a mystery.

"Are we almost there?" I asked.

"Almost," Cleo assured me with a laugh. "You sound like my niece, by the way. She's five."

"Hey!" I really couldn't mount a stronger defense since she was completely right. "Can't you at least give me a hint where we're heading?"

"I'm not giving the game away." She bumped my shoulder with hers and then added cryptically, "Not yet, at any rate."

"You can be so maddening." My smile was wide as I said this, and my stomach flip-flopped as she beamed a similar grin back at me.

"You'll figure it out soon enough."

Just after she said this, a massive dome came into view. If I'd had any doubts what it was, the cross on its top provided a big hint. "Is that St. Paul's? I thought you said we wouldn't have time to fit it in today."

"That's because I thought you were planning to cut the day short and drag us back to the shop for a PowerPoint presentation."

"Would you really have sat through the whole thing if I had?"

"Yes." Cleo's eyes twinkled with that particular brand of mischief I'd come to associate with her. "But only out of spite."

"In that case, I'm glad for both of us that you talked me out of it."

"So am I." Her tone was like warm honey, and for a moment, my insides became every bit as gooey, but then her expression shifted into tour guide mode once more. "If we want to make it to the top, we really need to get moving."

I eyed the towering structure with trepidation. "What do you mean the top?"

"See up there?" Cleo pointed to the very tip-top. I had to squint but was shocked when I spied outlines of tiny people standing on a platform at the top of the dome.

"That's high." I swallowed.

"More than five hundred steps up." She pointed, moving her hand higher to highlight the climb.

"Then…" Her finger dove downward as she made a whistling sound.

"Let's hope the climb down isn't as dramatic as you've made it look in your illustration. I'm way too young to die."

"Too cute, too," she said, or at least that's what my ears told me I'd heard above the sudden din of traffic as a bus pulled away from the curb, angering a cab driver, who laid on his horn.

Had she intended for me to hear that comment?

My insides were going all gooey yet again.

We entered the cathedral and immediately arrived at a bag search. There weren't many people around, though that wasn't a surprise given that it was a Friday afternoon in late November, so we got through quickly. It struck me as odd to have security at a church entrance, and I said as much to Cleo.

"Yes, well." Cleo chuckled quietly, casting a glance at the security guard and lowering her voice to barely a whisper. "Suffragettes planted a bomb under the Bishop's throne in 1913, so you can't be too careful."

My eyes grew wide. "Did it explode?"

"No. It was found in time. It's fitting, though, I think, that a hundred-odd years later, the bishop who sits there now is a woman."

"Remarkable," I replied, wondering what the women who'd tried to destroy the throne would've thought of that. My eyes traveled upward, taking in the glittering gold accents on white marble walls. As we walked, the black and white checkered floor made my head woozy.

We reached the center of the church where a pattern reminiscent of a compass rose formed a massive circle on the floor. Without saying a word, Cleo pointed up. I tilted my head and discovered we were beneath the giant dome, a view so dizzying I had to reach for her arm to steady myself.

"Impressive, yes?" Cleo grinned, clearly amused at my show of weakness. As we started toward the other end of the cathedral, she kept my hand tucked into the crook of her elbow, and I wasn't about to call attention to the fact, lest she realize it and pull away.

"There was another close call in 1940, when a bomb fell during a night raid and became lodged nearly ten meters deep in the road just outside the Cathedral. It took a crew of men three days to dig it out, all the while knowing at any minute it could detonate."

A shiver traveled down my spine. "Can you imagine? I'm not sure I could be that brave."

"Honestly, it's a miracle this place survived the war," Cleo said. "Before we head upstairs, you must see the American Memorial Chapel. While most of the cathedral remained intact, the area around the high altar was destroyed during the blitz. See the stained-glass windows? They contain symbols of all fifty states to honor the twenty-eight thousand American soldiers who were stationed in the UK and died in the war."

Tears stung my eyes as I studied the three brightly-colored windows. Looking closely, I could make out George Washington's head and an American eagle surrounding the more traditional religious imagery in the centers of the windows.

Cleo glanced at her watch. "I don't mean to rush you, but we need to hurry if we're to make it all the way to the Golden Gallery in time."

"These are the stairs you warned me about?" I asked when we reached the spiral staircase. It was wide, and the grade didn't require much lifting of our feet. "It's so gradual. I can't imagine it will take that long to reach the top."

"Trust me; it gets harder the higher we go."

We continued upward at a rapid pace, occasionally having to go single file to make way for someone coming down. Their red faces and obvious looks of relief at nearing the bottom told me Cleo wasn't joking about the increased difficulty ahead. True enough, the stairs got a bit more challenging but nothing too bad.

"Are we almost there?" I wasn't even out of breath yet.

"Not even close, but our first stop is coming up at the Whispering Gallery."

We stepped into a circular balcony of sorts that offered a spectacular view of the nave below, although my vision swirled somewhat as I took in the height. "Why is it called—what'd you say it was again?"

"Whispering gallery. There's a bit too much

ambient noise at the moment, but when it's still, if you say something up here, everyone along the curved wall can hear it."

A bench circumnavigated the gallery. I took a seat, pressing my ear to the wall, but I couldn't discern what I was hearing from all the commotion of tourists talking and laughing.

"I don't suggest discussing a plot against the church or anything." Cleo rocked onto her heels. "How are the legs? Still able to keep going?"

"Just about. You go ahead. I'll catch up in a moment."

I eased my phone from my pocket, my heart contracting as she continued around the circle and the distance between us grew. There'd been no word from Glory to clarify what was going on between us. The farther from me Cleo became, the harder it was to watch and the more conflicted I became. As fickle as it was, my heart's desire at that moment was to spend every minute of the time I had left in London with this woman.

"I wish it could be you," I whispered.

On the other side of the gallery, Cleo paused. My stomach plummeted as I recalled how this gallery had gotten its name. Had she heard me? A second later she was moving again without so much as a backward glance. I stood and quickly joined Cleo at the stairs. When I did, nothing about her seemed any different than before. Chances were I was in the clear.

The stairs beyond the Whispering Gallery started to narrow, not exactly comfortable, but not bad enough to set off my claustrophobia. Even so, I was relieved when a breeze tickled my cheeks.

"Did we make it?" I asked.

"We can get a view here," Cleo answered, "but there's another level above."

We stepped outside, and the fresh air was a relief, although my legs were starting to get shaky.

Cleo checked her watch, frown lines creasing her brow. "Are you ready to keep going? We don't have much time."

I groaned but waved for her to lead the way.

We started up a metal spiral staircase, both of us huffing and puffing now. We reached a platform, but the respite was brief, as there were more stairs.

Another platform. More stairs.

There was a sign warning me to mind my head, but I was more concerned about my wheezing lungs and the burning in my calves. Fortunately, the stairs straightened out after that and just in time because my vision was really going wobbly. Unfortunately, the space drastically narrowed to the point I had to hunch.

"Have I mentioned I don't like cramped spaces?" I said, unable to hide the shakiness in my voice.

"No, you didn't. Are you okay?"

"Hanging in," I assured her, praying that would be the case.

Finally, we made it to the top, and I had never been

more excited to suck in fresh air and to no longer be squashed in a cement tube like I was the human version of toothpaste. A narrow stone doorway stood in front of us, opening to the gold-tinged sky beyond.

"Right through there is the Golden Gallery. It's the best view of London you can get." Cleo motioned for me to pass in front of her. "And we've made it with no time to spare."

"For what?"

"The surprise I promised."

"Visiting St. Paul's wasn't the surprise?"

Cleo laughed as she gave me a gentle nudge toward the doorway.

That was when I saw it.

The sun, a glowing orb of fire, hovered at the base of the horizon, beside the perfect circle of the London Eye.

"Look at the sky," I gasped. The color was indescribable, containing every shade of purple, pink, and orange, reflecting off of puffy gray clouds. As I took a step onto the narrow walkway with its metal railing that seemed wholly inadequate to the task of keeping us from plummeting to our deaths, the cathedral clock bells began to chime. I jumped, letting out a squeak, and would have scurried back inside if Cleo hadn't stood in my way.

"Four o'clock," Cleo said, putting her arm around me to guide me to the railing. "Sunset is in precisely three minutes."

We were the only visitors there, and it was little wonder. Despite the ethereal beauty of the view at that hour, the light was rapidly fading, and the whipping wind had lowered the temperature by several degrees.

"Keep moving," said the surly man whose job it was to monitor the gallery, and who clearly didn't want us dillydallying, even though there was no one else there to care.

"Come on." Cleo took my hand in hers, the warmth of her skin instantly dispelling any notion of being cold. "We can make it all the way around in time to catch the sun disappearing over the horizon."

Cleo said this like the task at hand was no big deal, but apparently, she did not share my fear of heights. After fewer than a dozen steps, I was trembling from head to toe.

"Cold?" Cleo asked.

I shook my head. "Terrified."

"Here. I'll keep you safe."

Still behind me, Cleo pressed her body to mine, urging me forward one inch at a time as we made our way around the top. Her sense of timing was impeccable. As we came back around to where we'd started, the last rays of sun sank out of sight, leaving only the gorgeous painted sky.

Without thinking, I turned and found myself chest to chest with Cleo. Her lips were so close I could nearly taste them. My heart pounded so loudly it drowned out the sound of the wind. It was the perfect moment, holding all the promise of a perfect kiss.

Before I could act, a gust of wind left me unsteady. I yelped as I grabbed for the railing, shutting my eyes. "Oh, God! I don't want to die."

The security guard poked his head out of the doorway with a scowl. "Keep moving."

I spun forward again, stumbling toward the doorway. While Cleo's timing may have been impeccable, mine most certainly was not.

CHAPTER TWENTY-SIX

THE DESCENT from the Golden Gallery was faster than the climb up, aided in part by the heaviness of my heart. With the magical moment lost, cold reality was setting in.

"Shall we go for a cocktail nearby?" Cleo asked when we had exited the cathedral. My pulse quickened, but then she added, "I'd like to discuss my proposal in more detail."

It hit me like a shot to the gut.

What did I really think was going to happen here? Despite whatever connection I'd felt between us, my relationship with Cleo was first and foremost a business arrangement. More specifically, her business was failing, and mine, as far as Triple B was concerned, was coming to an end. I'd allowed my romantic imagination to run away with me for most of the day, but now it was time to face facts.

"I'm sorry," I said, forcing my tone to remain neutral so as not to reveal the anguish inside. "I don't think I'm the person for the job."

"You're the only person I know, Marley," Cleo argued, which did nothing to boost my confidence. Just because she didn't know anyone else didn't mean I wasn't going to fail at the nearly impossible task she wanted me to do.

"I'm sorry," I repeated. "I'm not a miracle worker."

"What will you do, then? Continue working for Triple B?" she asked, her expression filled with sadness.

"No. I can't do that. Move back home, maybe," I said. "Mom would like that, anyway."

"Wouldn't you rather move to London and help turn Braithwaite's around?"

"I don't have a work permit," I said in reply.

What I didn't say was that I didn't think my heart could handle the disappointment of working with her, knowing my feelings were one-sided. And clearly, they were, or she would have kissed me at sunset instead of letting me stumble around and be chased off by a grumpy security guard. I couldn't give voice to that because I was a coward in addition to being an utter fool.

"Marley—"

"I really should go. It's been a pleasure meeting you." I stuck out my hand.

"Is this really goodbye?" When I nodded, Cleo took my hand and gave it a shake. "Very well. Good luck to you."

"And you." I turned quickly so she wouldn't see the tears in my eyes.

CHAPTER TWENTY-SEVEN

I DIDN'T REMEMBER MUCH of the Tube ride back to the hotel. I kinda remember being on a train and tumbling out onto the sidewalk, but if you asked me the steps I took, I wouldn't be able to tell you.

When I was on the train, I couldn't take my eyes off the map of the stops as I held onto the pole to avoid swaying into other passengers. After a wonderful day spent exploring a small sliver of London, all I could think was how my time with Cleo was over. While it had seemed like Cleo and I covered London from end to end on foot, the map informed me we had barely scratched the surface. There was still so much of London to uncover.

I could come back and do it on my own, but what was the point? Without Cleo, the prospect was drained of its appeal.

How was this happening? I wasn't the type to fall

madly in love in less than twenty-four hours. But, I felt like I'd known Cleo for so much longer than a day.

Now, I stood in my hotel room, staring at the phone in my hand.

Looks like I can make it after all. Seven o'clock at Westminster Pier?

I eyed my date night outfit, the one I'd laid out that morning with such great expectations. I wondered if I should cancel on Glory. Would that be the right thing to do? I wasn't sure anymore. My sudden and intense feelings for Cleo had me all muddled. I felt like a disloyal cad.

Technically, despite how I felt inside, I hadn't cheated. I racked my brain on a quest to identify three excellent reasons why this was the case.

First, Glory and I had never specifically declared we were in an exclusive relationship. In fact, we hadn't declared anything at all, aside from our strong liking of the other and desire to meet in person to see if the spark translated into real life.

Second, I hadn't kissed Cleo. I had wanted to. Really, really, really wanted to. But, I didn't. And, it was worth reminding myself one more time in case I'd forgotten, she hadn't kissed me.

Third, a large part of me wished I was meeting Cleo tonight instead of Glory.

Wait. That wasn't the proof I needed. That was the opposite of what I was looking for. Yet, it was the absolute truth.

I sank down onto the bed, covering my eyes with my hands as tears rolled down my cheeks. How could I get ready for a date when I couldn't even stop crying? Wasn't there a rule of some type, no date night with one woman while experiencing waterworks for someone else?

I was a terrible person. Utterly wretched.

On the other hand, how would Glory feel if I stood her up now?

That would make me feel even worse. No, I needed to dry my eyes, put on my clothes, and try to have an enjoyable night.

Simple, right?

I burst into tears again.

CHAPTER TWENTY-EIGHT

THE DOCK at Westminster Pier was filling up with excited people, all laughing, smiling, and looking as if they were about to embark on a grand cruise along the Thames. Meanwhile, despite having managed to pretty myself up a little and chase most of the redness from my eyes, deep down I felt as though I was headed toward banishment at the Tower of London. I kept imagining a Beefeater in a red and gold uniform with a black hat, dragging me from the boat while exclaiming, "Lock up this traitor of the heart!"

Or something along those lines.

I stood off to the side, standing awkwardly under a streetlamp, holding a hardcover copy of *Pride and Prejudice* along with a single red rose. It was possible, way back in the day, that I'd suggested this as a way for Glory to recognize me because I'd watched one too many sappy romcoms.

Oh, how I wished I could get into a time machine and return to those heady days when we'd first started to correspond with one another. If only I could tell the me back then to turn down the job with Triple B. I would pay for my own flight and meet Glory the previous summer the way I should have, when I was all excited and aglow with possibilities.

Now, I had nothing but regret.

Glancing up, I caught a glimpse of a brightly-colored scarf that reminded me of a fortune-teller and made my insides turn fiery. Even while waiting for Glory, my mind and heart were seeking out Cleo. Of course, it wasn't her. I pictured her sitting in her charming bookshop, forlorn over its fate, the one I was leaving it to because I wasn't strong enough or brave enough to try.

Soon, she would be shuttering its door one final time.

Was it too much to hope part of Cleo's sadness involved me? No. She wasn't a sentimental fool, and even my runaway imagination couldn't be convinced that she cared one way or another about me.

The ship's crew undid the red rope, checking tickets, allowing people to board, and still there wasn't a sign of Glory.

As the crowd thinned, I started to wonder if Glory had gotten cold feet again.

An ironic laugh burbled out of me. It would be a fitting end to the day, wouldn't it? From two women to none, and me all alone on the Thames. Did I deserve anything else?

I wiped away a tear, looking at the revelers on the boat, getting drinks and claiming their spots outside to watch the ship pull away, or whatever the technical term was.

Undock? Launch? Sail?

Letting the book and rose fall to my sides, I flipped around, crestfallen.

All I needed to do was go back to the hotel, climb under the bed covers, and hope the sun did indeed come out again tomorrow. Cleo said it always did, but was she right?

"Carol?"

My body froze at the voice that came from behind me, calling out the name I'd given her. That voice, though. It sounded like—

"Are you coming or not?"

No. It can't be.

Ever so slowly, I turned around, and when I did, I had to blink not once but four times. Because, impossible as it seemed, it *was*.

There was Cleo, wearing her fortune-teller's scarf.

I managed to choke out, "How?"

CHAPTER TWENTY-NINE

"HURRY UP, LOVE," said the man with the red rope in his hand, waiting to clip it shut. "Get onboard now, or we'll leave you behind."

Cleo stepped forward and grabbed my hand, pulling me onto the gangway.

"But, how?" I repeated for what seemed like the millionth time.

"Let's get a drink and find a spot to chat," Cleo said as if this was completely normal. "I think I have some explaining to do."

We stood at the bar, Cleo holding up two fingers, and the bartender poured two glasses of red wine. I didn't want booze. I wanted answers. Had I fallen asleep at the hotel, and this was a dream? Maybe I was under a spell. Yes, that seemed like the only explanation.

When Cleo tried to hand me the glass of wine, my right hand clutched the book and my left grasped the rose. There was only one thing to do.

Laugh uncontrollably.

Cleo cocked her head to the side, smiling.

"There's a table by the window. Everyone else is outside. This way we can chat."

"Chat. Yes. Let's chat," I rambled. "Or maybe we should see if we can fly."

Cleo looked at me in alarm. "What on earth are you talking about?"

"Since I'm almost certainly asleep back at the hotel and having a very realistic dream, I might as well give it a try." I raised my arms, still holding onto the book and rose.

Cleo sat me down in a chair, prying the book from my hand.

I flinched as the edge of the book pinched my skin. "That felt real."

"How about this?" Cleo brushed a fingertip along the top of my hand, sending tingles up my arm.

"Also real." I gulped.

A man played a piano while a woman in a black cocktail dress started to sing a jazz tune, but I didn't know the name.

"That settles it, then. This must be real." Cleo smiled in that way of hers that conveyed I was adorable but also a little bit of an idiot, which I couldn't really dispute given all the evidence. Had I really said I wanted to try to fly to our table? "It can't be."

"Why?"

"Because you're not supposed to be here. I didn't tell you what my plans were this evening, yet here you are. Ergo, I have to be dreaming. Has this entire day been a dream?" I added. "It's been magical."

Cleo took a sip of her wine instead of speaking, which only reinforced the dream theory. But then she said something I wasn't expecting. "Of course, you told me what the plan was this evening."

"When?"

"I don't remember the exact day we first talked about this date, but you also sent me a text earlier this evening, asking me to reconsider showing up." Cleo searched my eyes, looking for something but obviously not finding it. "You still seem confused."

"Thoroughly," I concurred.

"Marley, *I'm* Glory."

"You look nothing like her." Okay, I'd never seen an actual photo of Glory that didn't play tricks with my mind, but her avatar had a starring role in many of my fantasies. I leaned forward, squinting as I tried to superimpose a one-inch square avatar of an Egyptian princess over Cleo's features, not feeling the least bit ridiculous.

"How do you know?"

"Because—okay, you have a good point." Then another thought slammed into my head, and I sat up straight, anger flooding my central nervous system. "This whole thing has been a setup. The entire day. You requested me to come to London. You've made me look a fool!"

"That was never my intention." Cleo seemed to shrink three inches. "Let me explain, please."

"Explain what? I think I'm finally getting the whole picture of your deception."

"I wouldn't call it that."

"What would you call it?"

"Clarification." Cleo gazed into my eyes. "I needed to be sure."

"Of?"

"You. I needed to know you were who you claimed to be."

"Oh, that's rich, all things considered." The sting of betrayal was still fresh. "How long did you know?"

"Are you sure you don't want some of your wine?" She scooted the glass closer to my hand, but I pushed it away.

"I want answers."

"Okay." Cleo inhaled a deep breath. "You must understand that prior to my mum turning the shop over to me, Triple B had tried many unsavory methods to get a meeting with my mother. When I realized Carol, the woman I was falling for online, was also an employee of Triple B, I suspected the company was up to its old tricks, and you were a plant to fool me."

"Me? You think I joined the online book club to fool you?" I placed a hand on my chest. "Why would you think that about me?"

"It wasn't personal. It was Triple B I didn't trust." Cleo took another sip of wine. "I needed to know you were real and not a spy."

"Oh, now I'm a spy? This is utterly ridiculous."

"Not if you knew the extent of your company's unsavory reputation."

"What about Cleo Braithwaite's reputation as a heartless and terrifying maven of the book world?" I countered.

"I told you before," Cleo said quietly, "that was my mother."

"I never understood why you requested me specifically." I slapped my palm against my forehead as the truth hit me. My heart was cleaving into two. "I've been such a fool. This entire time, you were playing a game. Well done, Cleo Braithwaite. You're every bit as ruthless as they said you were. Your mother would be proud."

"Please don't look that way. Hear me out," Cleo pleaded.

"It was all a lie. Right from the start. It serves me right for falling in love with an avatar."

"No!" She held a hand in the air as if to stop me

from speaking. "Not at the start. From the moment we started chatting, I was smitten with Carol, a booklover who found me clever and witty."

I was still angry, like really fucking mad, but had she said she was smitten? I pressed my lips together and resolved to hear her out. We were stuck on a boat. It wasn't like I could storm away.

"You probably don't remember this, but you let a little detail slip in one of our chats about how you were in Chicago for a business deal. As it happens, I'm friends with the owner of that shop, and she told me all about your meeting."

"What did she say?"

"That Triple B was every bit the scoundrel we believed the company to be. But she said the representative was a lovely woman who didn't seem at all terrible and was a real booklover who went on and on about this online book club. It sounded like the one I'd told her about one time."

"I do remember that," I conceded. "Except for the scoundrel part."

"I realize now that you didn't know that part. But think about how it looked to me then. It didn't take much sleuthing to realize the woman I was falling in love with online worked for the evil corporation who wanted to destroy my family business."

"Uh-huh." *Had she said falling in love with? Had I said it myself earlier?*

"I determined the only way to solve the mystery of whether or not I was the victim of corporate espionage or sick fate was to get Triple B to send you here. I needed to know if you were a company shark or truly the booklover I had so much in common with."

Setting down my wineglass, I folded my arms across my chest. "Exactly how were you going to determine this?"

"My first goal was to get you away from the shop and your proposal. I figured if you agreed to go sightseeing with me, there was a better chance you at least had the same personality as your online persona."

"Which is?"

"Someone who enjoys life. Who finds the littlest things fascinating. Which, you do. I knew that the moment you rammed into me because you were too busy looking at Big Ben."

"If that's true, why didn't you tell me right then and there what was going on?" A tear spilled down my cheek.

"I wasn't ready to."

"Why?"

"You seemed convinced Triple B was legit. I couldn't reconcile that fact with how much you clearly love books."

"I didn't know how bad the company was. When I interviewed for the job, we visited the first bookstore Triple B purchased, right in the heart of New York

City. It was the cutest thing I'd ever seen. Well, until I walked into your shop, that is."

"I think in the beginning, Triple B wasn't exactly the vulture it is now. Years ago, Mum was tempted. But, after I traveled the US a bit more, checking out some of their acquisitions, I told her not to."

"You haven't explained what your end game was for today. How exactly did you envision it would turn out?"

"I'm afraid that's where my plan got a little fuzzy. We clicked right from the start, and then I didn't know how to confess. We were having so much fun, and I didn't want you to look at me the way you are now."

"How am I looking at you now?" I asked, my voice barely above a whisper.

"With disappointment."

"Can you blame me? You played me for a fool. I give you credit for canceling the date. Was all the lying not dramatic enough?"

"That's not why I canceled. I didn't know how to fix things. I can see now it was a horrible thing to do." Cleo took each of my hands into hers. "I'm so very sorry, Marley. I never wanted to hurt you."

"What did you want?" I demanded. "After you decided I wasn't a spy, that is."

"I can tell you what I didn't want. I didn't want to lose our connection."

"Then why did you—or rather, Glory—try to cancel our date?"

"Because I was hoping that with Glory out of the way, I would be able to convince you to go out with me instead."

"But you are Glory, so you basically canceled a date with me in order to convince me to go on the exact same date? Is there a word for that? Duplicitous?" That didn't sound right.

"It's why I decided to take you to St. Paul's. What could be more romantic than a first kiss at sunset with a view of London? But I didn't count on you being so afraid of heights or that the security guard would have such poor timing." Cleo sighed.

"You're an idiot." My tone still held a hint of anger but also humor.

"I really am. A desperate one who wants you to say everything will be okay. Not right away but with time. I won't give up, you know. You mean too much to me."

"Part of me wants to," I confessed. "But, I hate liars."

"I completely understand, and if I were in your shoes, I'd tell me to jump ship. Literally."

"The water is so dark." I shivered from the thought and then let out an anguished sigh. "Why did you offer me a job?"

"That just came to me."

"Does that mean you don't want my help with the shop?"

"Oh, I do, but when I proposed it earlier today, I was still of the mind that I wouldn't have to confess I was Glory. Having you work with me—honestly, I want to be near you, always. I thought, over time, you'd fall for the real me. We were connecting, like we'd known each other for an eternity."

"We have."

"Yes, that's true. It's probably best things turned out this way. At least you know the full truth now. I don't think I'd want you not to know. Even if it means you decide never to speak to me again."

I sighed. "I don't like the sound of that."

"For the record, neither do I."

"What to do?" I studied her eyes for an answer.

"The ball's in your court, as you Americans say."

"I'm still mad."

"As you should be."

"The day you planned, it included a lot of things I wanted to see."

"It's possible I intentionally pumped you for information."

"Another thing I should be mad about." I admit I didn't sound angry at all.

"Should be?" Her voice was downright pleading.

"It was such a lovely day. A few hiccups but also very lovely."

"It really was."

"What should I do?"

"You're asking me?" She placed a hand over her heart.

"I am. How many times have I asked for your guidance online?"

"A lot, but… I can't believe I'm saying this, but I can't tell you what to do. I want to say forgive me. I only wanted the Triple B issue to disappear. Not you. If I was in your shoes, though, I'm not sure what I would do." She let out a huff of air. "I really didn't put enough thought into this portion of my plan. I'm so sorry, Marley. So, so, so sorry." Her bottom lip quivered. It tore through me.

"Do you promise to tell me the truth from now on?"

"Absolutely." Cleo made a cross over her heart.

"In that case, you can start with this. What is black pudding?"

She burst into laughter. "That's your first question?"

"Honestly, it was the only thing I could think of. I'm sure once all of this settles in my mind—which will take time, lots and lots of time—I'll have many more questions."

"You really want to know?" She eyed me with caution.

"Is it that bad?"

"Depends."

I shrank back but remained resolved. "Go on. It's my turn to test you like you've been testing me all day."

"It's blood sausage."

I gaped at her as that washed over me until I was finally able to say, "I guess that's fitting."

"What do you mean?"

"I feel like my heart is bleeding out."

"Oh, Marley." Cleo took me into her arms, holding me close, and I had no desire to fight her off. In fact, letting go of me was the last thing I wanted her to do.

CHAPTER THIRTY

"THE BRIDGE IS OPENING!" a voice called out. People hustled and bustled all around us, leaving me to wonder when they'd all come inside the boat. The last I remembered, we'd had the dining area to ourselves.

"What bridge?" I asked, my head still pressed against Cleo's breast.

"Tower Bridge."

I pulled back. "The one I wanted to see open?"

"Yes." She swept loose hair off my face, back behind an ear. "This particular boat is tall enough that the bridge needs to be opened to allow it to pass. It's one of the selling points of this cruise."

I regarded her with an odd sense of awe. "You knew all along this was the plan tonight, and you didn't spill?"

"It was killing me not to. Now I'm hoping you don't want to kill me."

I narrowed my eyes. "The jury's still out."

Cleo donned a repentant expression. "Before you have me locked up in the Tower of London and executed for my treachery, let's at least go outside to watch the show."

"I won't say no to that part."

"But you might say yes to beheading me?" She glanced over her shoulder as she led me by the hand onto the deck.

"I'm not taking any options off the table quite yet." I was totally bluffing. Cleo was as good as forgiven already. However, she didn't need to know that quite yet. It was difficult for me to understand the pull this woman had on me. I knew I wouldn't be able to get the right words out. I basically asked God at St. Paul's for Cleo to be Glory, and my prayer had been answered.

Out on the deck, the sky above us was inky with a splattering of some clouds. Tower Bridge lay ahead, dazzling with white lights. As we drew closer, a purple glow reflected in the black water of the Thames. My breath caught as the middle of the bridge slowly pulled apart, each half rising upward to allow our boat to pass through. As we glided closer, the lights from the underside of the bridge twinkled like a million amethysts in the moonlight.

"This is amazing," I whispered.

Cleo had her eyes on me. "It is."

"You aren't even looking at it."

"I'm seeing exactly what I want."

"Which is?"

"You, Marley Royce. Not Carol, not the potential corporate spy, but you, the woman I spent one of the best days of my life with today." She took a deep breath. "Is it too late, though?"

"It should be." My jaw hardened as I recalled all that we'd gone through. "I hate liars. Always have. Glory and Carol were nothing but a lie." Not that I wanted to admit my role in the shenanigans, but I had used an alias. My fib didn't match Cleo's, but I hadn't been entirely straightforward.

"I understand." Briefly her eyes fell, but with steely nerve, she met my stare again. "At least we'll always have Tower Bridge."

I glanced at the bridge with its two halves standing at attention. The boat was almost underneath the bridge. It was now or never to see what the future held.

"I'm glad we didn't kiss at the top of St. Paul's," I told her, "because there was still your lie between us. But now—"

"But now?" Hope sprang to life in Cleo's eyes.

I glanced upward at the purple bridge directly overhead, feeling as if London itself was blessing my next move.

I kissed her, softly and sweetly.

Cleo kissed me back just as sweetly, wrapping her arms around my neck. I circled mine around her waist, pulling her closer.

Briefly, our lips parted, and I said, "It's nice to meet you, Cleo Braithwaite."

"It's lovely to make your acquaintance, Marley Royce."

We kissed again, our future as bright as the lights on the river.

EPILOGUE

"THIS IS the cutest thing I've seen." I circled the three-foot squirrel painted in plaid colors. "I didn't want to see *The Adventures of Earl* until I saw this little guy."

"Not so little." Cleo took a step back, pursing her lips.

"You're not fooling me. Not one bit. You love having one of the promotional squirrels in the shop, and it's good for business, too. It's bringing in more kids with their moms, not to mention so many tourists—"

"Tourists are very annoying," Cleo butted in. "Especially the American ones. Talking loudly and acting like they own the place." She lumbered about, stomping her feet in an imitation of said American tourists.

I ignored her as best as I could. I would never

admit it out loud, but even when mocking my people, I found her sexy.

"As I was saying, no one can have a bad day at work with this little guy exuding his British charm. He even has a monocle and cane. Come on. Admit it. He's the cutest thing you've ever seen."

"I'll admit nothing of the sort, but I'll shout from the rooftops that you're adorable." Cleo wrapped her arms around my waist, immediately redeeming herself for bashing my fellow Americans moments before. "And sexy. Can we call it a day and...?" She quirked her eyebrow in that special way she had that never failed to drive me mad.

"The shop hasn't even opened!" I protested but only because one of us had to be the adult, and clearly, it wasn't going to be her.

Cleo pouted. "When did you become married to the store?"

Before I could answer, Sheila burst in from the back of the store. "We're out of Earl books." When her eyes locked on Earl the Squirrel, that schoolmarm facade of hers, the one that had terrified me the first day we'd met, melted away. "I love him."

"You see? He's the best thing that ever happened to this place!" I jabbed the air with my finger to emphasize my point and then turned to Sheila. "We got a box in yesterday. I'll get them."

Before I slipped into the back, I overheard Sheila say, "Isn't it lovely how busy the store's been? A year ago, I thought we were done for, but Marley's turned it around."

"That she has!" Cleo's voice brimmed with pride, making the butterflies flutter in my belly. The woman might be grumpy about a squirrel statue, but when it came to the store's recent success, Cleo heaped all the credit onto my bookstore acumen. Probably more than I deserved if I were honest about it. Really, it was the store itself that pulled customers in. I'd just given it the right nudge here and there to bring in the punters, as Cleo loved to say.

"Now, where is that box? I could have sworn it was right here." I glanced about the storeroom.

"Looking for your marbles?" Cleo offered up a mischievous grin as she joined me in the back room.

I tripped over a box, which sadly wasn't the one I needed.

"Careful!" Cleo rushed to steady me.

"Stop with all your flirting, then," I pretended to scold. "You know what it does to me."

She flashed a wicked grin. "Why do you think I do it?"

"To kill me, obviously. It's a Saturday. We can't leave Sheila to fend for herself. So, if you could temper your powers of seduction until five," I pleaded, "I'd be truly grateful."

"This is the part I don't like about having an American business partner. The incessant need to work." There was that grin again, as if letting me know that if

I expected her to behave, she wasn't going to make it easy.

"Not going to work." I lied, avoiding so much as a glance in her direction since I knew that was all it would take for me to lose my resolve. "Help me find the box. It was right here, yesterday." I stomped the gray floor.

"Are you sure?"

"Of course, I'm sure. I remember putting it here because I knew we needed the books. The author of *The Adventures of Earl* is coming in today for a reading, and we're raffling off tickets to the movie premier."

"Did you look over there?" Cleo pointed to the spot in the backroom none of us ever wanted to venture into with all the crap that had accumulated since the days of Charles Dickens. If I hadn't seen the man's grave myself at Westminster, I'd swear his bones could've been hiding back there, and none of us would've known.

"You know as well as I do I would never place something we need over there." I shuddered, hoping to make my point.

"Maybe Earl comes to life at night and moves things around. Another reason to hate the overgrown rat."

I crossed my arms, tilting my head to one side. "Will you please help me?"

"I'm trying to do more than that!" Cleo grabbed my hand and dragged me behind the curtain.

I snapped my eyes shut.

"You have to open them to see." She laughed.

"It scares me in here."

"Trust me," Cleo whispered, sending shockwaves through my core and boosting my courage enough to comply.

I cracked one eye open. Overcome with shock, the other eye flew open wide. "What the holy hell?" I took in the space, which was sparkling. "Who cleaned it?"

"I did. And not only that, look what I found." Cleo pointed to a bookstand where a red book with gold lettering set my heart palpitating.

"Is this what I think it is?" I approached the book but didn't dare open it.

"Depends. Do you think it's a first edition of *A Christmas Carol* that was signed to my great-great-great grandfather by Charles Dickens in 1843?"

My throat went dry. "Are you telling me this has been here the entire time?"

"Apparently so." Cleo shrugged as if she was used to finding treasures like this every time she cleaned her house. "Want to read it?"

"It should be... I don't even know. Under glass, maybe?"

"You're no fun. You know that?"

"I'm serious, Cleo. We can't keep it here."

"I know." She shuffled her feet. "I've contacted the British Library already. I thought we could donate it—"

My mouth dropped open. "Do you know how much that's worth?"

"Fifty thousand pounds at the least, I should think. But we—"

"Could get some really good publicity for the shop," I suggested. "That's brilliant."

"Actually, I thought we could tell the library it's a gift from Marley and Cleo Braithwaite-Royce."

I laughed until what she'd said sunk in. "Hold on. Are you…?"

"Suggesting we get married?" Cleo's eyes brimmed. "I believe I am."

"There's just one problem." I eyed the book again, holding up my left hand and turning it from side to side. "How do I put a book on my finger?"

"That is a problem, but I may have an alternative. Would this do?" Cleo presented me with an antique box. "It belonged to my great-grandmother."

My breath caught as I opened the box to find a small diamond set in white gold filigree nestled into the velvet cushion inside. My hands began to shake so much there was no way I could remove the ring from the box or even attempt to slide it on.

"You haven't said yes or no." Cleo's eyes were wide with anticipation. Or was that fear? Instantly, my senses returned to me. Clutching the box, I threw my arms around Cleo's neck.

"Yes, yes, yes!" Still holding tightly to both her and

the ring, I only barely managed to wipe a tear as it rolled down my cheek.

"Thank goodness, because if you'd said no, it would be beyond awkward running this shop together." Cleo laughed at her own joke.

"You're such a dork, sometimes," I said into her ear.

"I thought you loved my quirkiness."

"Oh, I do," I assured her, unclasping my arms and taking a small step back. "But I reserve the right to point it out forever now."

"I can live with that." Taking the tiny box from my hand, Cleo plucked the ring from its cushion. She grasped my hand and slid it onto my finger. "A perfect fit."

"In every way," I said.

And then I kissed her.

A HUGE THANK YOU!

First, thanks so much for reading *The Proposal*. I thoroughly enjoyed writing this story and bringing Marley and Cleo to life. I have to admit I wish I could have joined them on their walking tour. When travel becomes a thing again, I'm sure I'll head to my favorite pub along their route and raise a glass to them.

I've published more than twenty novels, and I still find it simply amazing people read my stories. When I hit publish on my first book back in 2013, after staring at the publish button for several days before I worked up the nerve to finally press it, I had no idea what would happen.

Many years later, I still panic when I'm about to publish a new project, but it's because of your support that I find the courage to do it. My publishing career has been a wonderful journey, and I wouldn't be where I am today without you cheering me on.

If you enjoyed the story, I would really appreciate a review. Even short reviews help immensely.

Finally, if you want to stay in touch, sign up for my newsletter. I'll send you a free copy of *A Woman Lost*, book 1 in the A Woman Lost series, plus the bonus chapters and *Tropical Heat* (a short story) that are exclusive to subscribers. And, you'll be able to enter monthly giveaways to win one of my books.

You'll also be one of the firsts to hear about many of my misadventures, like the time I accidentally ordered thirty pounds of oranges instead of five. To be honest, that stuff happens to me a lot, which explains why I own three of the exact same *Nice Tits* T-shirt. In case you're wondering, the shirt has pictures of the different tits of the bird variety, because I have some pride.

Here's the link to join: http://eepurl.com/hhBhXX

ABOUT THE AUTHOR

TB Markinson is an American who's recently returned to the US after a seven-year stint in the UK and Ireland. When she isn't writing, she's traveling the world, watching sports on the telly, visiting pubs in New England, or reading. Not necessarily in that order.

Her novels have hit Amazon bestseller lists for lesbian fiction and lesbian romance. For a full listing of TB's novels, please visit her Amazon page.

Feel free to visit TB's website to say hello. On the *Lesbians Who Write* weekly podcast, she and Clare Lydon dish about the good, the bad, and the ugly of writing. TB also runs I Heart Lesfic, a place for authors and fans of lesfic to come together to celebrate and chat about lesbian fiction.

Want to learn more about TB. Hop over to her *About* page on her website for the juicy bits. Okay, it won't be all that titillating, but you'll find out more.

Printed in Great Britain
by Amazon